TO BEAD OR NOT TO BEAD

A Glass Bead Mystery

JANICE PEACOCK

Vetrai Press

Lafayette, California

2018

PRAISE FOR
TO BEAD OR NOT TO BEAD

"Janice Peacock brings down the house with her latest novel, *To Bead or Not to Bead*. Once again, the spotlight follows amateur sleuth Jax O'Connell as she tries to save the local community theater and solve a murder before the final curtain call. "Breaking a leg" is the least of her worries in this fun and intriguing story. The Bard would be proud!"
— **D.J. Lutz**, author of The Apple Pie Alibi, a Culinary Mystery

"Another bead-azzling mystery! Follow Jax and her friends as they uncover a dramatic murder that will leave you guessing until the very end."
— **J.J. Chow**, author of the Winston Wong Cozy Mysteries

"With *To Bead or Not to Bead*, Janice Peacock has crafted another gem in her Glass Bead Mystery series, with humor, quirky characters and a twisty plot. A fun cozy read."
— **Vickie Fee**, author of Liv and Di in Dixie mystery series

"Ms. Peacock continues to grow into the difficult role of writing a lasting and engaging cozy series. In her latest, *To Bead or Not to Bead*, we are drawn into the world of the theatre, where she highlights her gift of spinning an engrossing story."
— **Heather Haven**, multi-award winning author
of the Alvarez Family Murder Mysteries

"A fun, fast-paced cozy with twists and turns galore! Jax O'Connell is a tenacious amateur sleuth with just the right amount of spunk. Her latest adventure is an action-packed mystery that will keep you guessing until the end."
— **Marla Cooper**, author of the Kelsey McKenna Destination
Wedding Mysteries

For Kiera

ONE

FRANKIE LAWTON stood in the middle of the stage screaming at his volunteers. Dressed in a scarlet suit, with a shock of white hair on his head, he reminded me of Santa—except for his attitude, which was somewhere between bossy and shrill—definitely not jolly. The only thing he was missing was a white beard; the only thing I wished he was missing was his bright red bullhorn.

"You, over there! That column needs to be downstage left," Frankie shouted. "And you! Yes, you! Do not let that fall over—it's fragile for chrissake!" This time he was yelling at me, and I didn't like it one bit.

"I'm doing the best I can! This thing is heavy," I said, mostly to myself, setting down a faux marble column near the front of the stage. Tessa, who was assigned the unglamorous job of using the push broom, swept up next to me.

"When we said we'd volunteer for this event, I didn't think that meant we'd be doing all this manual labor. I thought we'd be helping the models get ready for their spin on the runway," she said.

"It was your idea to volunteer, so I don't want to hear it," I said, wiping a trickle of sweat from my forehead.

Tessa, my best friend since kindergarten, had roped me into

helping at the inaugural auction and fashion show fundraiser for
the Homeless Advocacy Team, also known as HAT, a nonprofit that
helped teens and young adults find jobs and permanent shelter.
When she asked me to help, I knew I had to say yes. One thing I'd
learned in all of my years of knowing Tessa: I couldn't tell her no,
and neither could anyone else.

The gala was sponsored in part by the high school Tessa's
daughters attended. Her girls, Izzy and Ashley, had volunteered to be
models in the fashion show and would be wearing clothes supplied
by local boutiques. While Tessa was tiny, her girls had inherited their
height from their father. Both were tall with long legs, looking nearly
coltish as they walked around the stage. In addition to the outfits,
the girls would be wearing necklaces designed by Frankie Lawton, a
world-renowned jewelry designer. I'd first met Frankie last spring at
the grand opening of Aztec Beads, our local bead shop. At the time,
he'd placed a huge order for my handmade glass beads, and that had
helped launch my career as a professional artist.

Frankie Lawton had been assigned the role of Master of
Ceremonies, but so far he seemed to be acting more like Master of
the Universe. He was the closest thing we had to a local celebrity,
given that he'd rubbed elbows with the likes of Elton John and
Hillary Clinton, creating gorgeous and often oversized jewelry
that coordinated with their fashionable pantsuits. He would be
an entertaining host for the event, but I didn't like his attitude as
we prepared.

Today was our first day of rehearsal for the event, which
was taking place in just a few days at the Chanticleer Theater in
downtown Seattle, Washington. The theater had once been exquisite.
Gilt panels with curlicued corners festooned each wall. Crystal
lighting fixtures adorned the high ceiling, although some had been
replaced or masked by less beautiful, but more practical, equipment
meant to light the stage during the community theater plays that the
Chanticleer now presented. The venue was impressive, even though
it was showing signs of age, with 300 elegantly faded red velvet
seats arching away from the curved front of the stage.

While we were there to produce a fashion show and auction, the stage was also being used for something much more dramatic—a production of Shakespeare's *Hamlet*. The play's set was a 1980s-era rock star mansion, complete with neon-colored furniture, gold records lining the walls, and a little too much animal print to be tasteful. My neighbor Val would have loved it, since she had a penchant for faux zebra. Recently, several theater companies had resorted to modern reboots of classics to pull in crowds. I was worried this wacky modern-yet-retro version of the play would be a disaster. To me, the whole thing looked gaudy, but I supposed if the actors could pull it off, it might be a way to get people into the theater and exposed to the works of Shakespeare. As long as Hamlet didn't have a green Mohawk, it might work. But what did I know? While I knew a lot about glass, and handmade glass beads in particular, I didn't know much about theater.

To get our attention, Frankie was clapping his hands together above his head like a flamenco dancer. When no one paid the slightest bit of attention, he grabbed the bullhorn again.

"Attention! Everyone! Please!" We all stopped in our tracks, reacting to Frankie's amplified shouts. "Let's get everything cleared off the stage!" The tired volunteers each grabbed the set piece they'd brought out. For me, that meant lugging the faux marble pedestal backstage and putting it where I'd be able to find it again later. After sliding it into position in the wings, I turned and slammed into a tall, stork-like man.

"Watch out! You nearly spilled my coffee," the man hissed, the fine lines in his gaunt face pulled into a grimace. He cupped his hand over the top of his mug so it wouldn't splash on his perfectly pressed white Oxford shirt. I noticed the slightest tremor in his hands.

"Oh! I'm so sorry. I didn't see you there," I said to the man as I backed out of his way.

"You simply can't be moving so quickly backstage. There's not much room back here."

"I'll be more careful next time. I'm Jax, by the way," I said, introducing myself. I didn't extend my hand to shake, since both of his hands were busy protecting his coffee cup.

"Austin Greer. I own the place, so if you've got any complaints, come and see me," he said. I'd heard of Austin Greer, of course. He was a well-known philanthropist in Seattle, and his wife, Amanda, was a retired film actress who had been a big deal in the 1970s, when she starred in several blockbuster movies, including a stint as a Bond girl in one of the James Bond films. I wondered why on earth he'd think I'd have any complaints. He glanced at the necklace I was wearing, which featured a set of purple glass beads with light blue polka dots. Austin shifted gears from surly to pleasant. "Say, that's a nice necklace. Did you get that around here?"

"Thanks. Actually, it's my own design. I melt glass with a torch to make the beads."

"Do you ever work with other jewelry designers?"

"As a matter of fact, I do. Frankie Lawton ordered quite a few beads from me last spring."

"You should talk with my wife. She's a bead importer and designs her own jewelry. Maybe she'd be interested in some of your work. Just give her a call. You can take some things over to our house. She doesn't get out much."

"Sure. Do you want to text me her phone number?" I asked, pulling my phone from my purse, ready to confirm receipt of his message.

"Sorry, I don't carry a phone. Never could figure out why anyone would want to have people calling at all times of the day and night. All those bings and bongs—it would drive me batty." Mr. Greer beckoned a young woman in a gray blazer and slacks who was standing in the wings. Within seconds, she was at his side.

"Yes, Mr. Greer? How can I help you?" the woman asked.

"Ah, yes. Nika, this is Jackie," Austin said.

"Actually, it's Jax," I said, correcting him.

"Nika is my assistant and one of the wonderful young people who was helped by the Homeless Advocacy Team. Isn't that right?" Mr. Greer looked from me to Nika with a paternal smile.

"That's right, Mr. Greer," she responded. Although she was

smiling, I detected some discomfort in her stance.

"I think my wife would be very interested in seeing Jackie's beads and possibly making a purchase. Will you get in touch with Amanda and make an appointment for them to meet?" he asked Nika.

"Sure, my pleasure," Nika said as Mr. Greer sauntered off.

Turning, belatedly, he added, "Nice to meet you, Jackie."

I sighed internally. Actually, it may have been audible. Even so, Nika didn't seem to notice.

"I'll call you with an appointment time after I've had the opportunity to call Mrs. Greer. What's your number?" Nika asked.

I dug through my handbag looking for a business card. Finally, I found one and handed it to Nika. She assured me that she'd be in touch and dashed off to catch up with Mr. Greer.

Frankie shouted at us to reset the stage with our set pieces, and we hauled our pillars back out to their designated spots for the umpteenth time. Earlier in the day, Frankie explained to us that we had to quickly set up the set pieces between the end of the fashion show and the start of the auction. At least with all this heavy lifting, I wouldn't need to go to the gym today—not that I ever did.

"That's better! You didn't look like a bunch of bumbling idiots this time. Everyone, please take a seat in the house," Frankie said. We all milled around, not knowing where to go. "Come on everyone, 'the house' is where the audience sits!" He muttered something that sounded a lot like "stupid amateurs," but I couldn't be certain. Fortunately, he didn't use his bullhorn, because if he had, it would have been a race between me, Tessa, and a few of the other volunteers to see who could grab it from him and smash it into a million pieces.

As Tessa and I took a seat in the front row, we admired the stage in front of us. Along each side of the stage were pedestals that would eventually hold all the auction items. These items had been donated by local businesses and included everything from spa packages and hot air balloon rides to theater tickets and cases of wine.

Hanging front and center above the stage was an art glass chandelier, its multi-colored glass orbs reflecting the theater lights surrounding it. It was the *piece de resistance* to be auctioned off as the final item at the gala and was expected to raise many thousands of dollars for the nonprofit. The chandelier was magnificent. It was made entirely of glass and created to coordinate with the cacophony of bright colors onstage. The artist who had created it, known simply as Vega, had designed the luminous piece for the play and Austin Greer had donated it to our auction.

"All right—" Frankie started, having found his bullhorn again. He was immediately interrupted by Austin Greer—who was the opposite of Frankie in almost every way except that they were more or less from the same species. Mr. Greer stepped up to Frankie and unceremoniously yanked the bullhorn from him. Frankie was clearly taken aback. He clutched at his red bow tie, shocked that this person would be so bold as to grab his beloved bullhorn.

"Ladies and," Mr. Greer looked into the audience to see if there were any men. There were not. "And, Frankie. As the director of the gala, let me say thank you for all you are doing to make this event a success." He turned and pointed the bullhorn at Frankie, who was standing a mere two feet away. "That being said, please remember, you are just the emcee. I call the shots." Frankie cringed from the amplified voice booming through the bullhorn.

"That's Austin Greer," Tessa said, nodding toward the man.

"I met him backstage. He was a little rude, definitely an odd bird," I replied. "But he liked my beads."

"You should hear the awful things the girls say about him," Tessa said with a sigh.

"Your girls don't like him?"

"Don't get me started. Izzy and Ashley say Mr. Greer is awful. Apparently, he's condescending and rude—yells when even the smallest thing goes wrong. They almost quit working on the project because of him."

"Could they simply be overreacting?" Tessa's daughters were known for their dramatics, and not only when they were on stage.

"Apparently, he treats Izzy, Ashley, and all the girls working with him like idiots. It sounds like he's a perfectionist. If the girls don't do everything to his unreasonable standards, he insults them."

"Sometimes they fall to pieces even about the smallest things," I said. And that was true. Tessa's daughters, while lovely, talented, and smart, were a handful. Tessa was constantly refereeing battles between the girls, and I had witnessed and intervened in my own fair share of arguments between them. I hoped the gala would provide an opportunity for the girls to come together peacefully and that Tessa wouldn't be too stressed out trying to deal with their issues.

Mr. Greer took a sip from his coffee mug and continued. "Now, Frankie, go get our models, will you?" Frankie nodded and scurried offstage, if it was possible for a 220-pound man to scurry, to fetch the models from the dressing room. Returning moments later, he asked the models to line up in the middle of the stage. Mr. Greer paced back and forth in front of the lineup, examining the girls as if they were army recruits. Izzy and Ashley were among the five high school girls nervously standing shoulder to shoulder, fists clenched tightly at their sides. None of them made eye contact with the man. "Now, girls, I'm going to show you how to walk like a high-fashion model. Everyone will get a chance to practice."

Mr. Greer pushed his mug into Nika's waiting hands, then strode to center stage, pausing along the way to pose. He looked absolutely ridiculous, twirling at the edge of the stage, his trousers fluttering slightly as he whipped around. He headed back toward center stage swishing his hips, trying his best to imitate a model you'd see during New York's Fashion Week.

"Do you think you can do it?" he asked the group. Immediately, all the girls started prancing downstage in an awkward stampede. "No. No. No! One at a time! One. At. A. Time!" The herd of girls stopped in their tracks. "Every one of you, get backstage, including you, Frankie. Then I'll call you out one by one." The girls all hustled backstage, then Mr. Greer called out the name of each girl, who entered stage right, crossed to the center, twirled, and exited into the wings on the left.

After everyone finished, Mr. Greer took one more spin around the stage, then stopped at its edge to address the volunteers in the audience. I spotted Frankie, still in the wings, his mouth pulled into a puckered frown.

"Now, everyone. I think we are done for the day. Please come back tomorrow at the same time. Four o'clock. And do not be late!" Mr. Greer said.

The teens re-appeared onstage, and Mr. Greer addressed them as well. "Models, if you would like to bring the shoes you plan on wearing with your outfits, that would be superb." He made a slow exit down the side stairs into the audience. Nika was right behind him, handing his mug back to him as they headed toward the lobby.

In the dressing room, on the left side of the stage beyond the wings, Tessa and I helped the girls organize all the clothing that would be used in the fashion show. The room was lined with racks of costumes from nearly every era I could think of. Shelves loaded with hats, wigs, and props hugged the ceiling. Fortunately, the theater staff had carved out space for us to use for our event, although it was tight.

"I swear, if my girls hung up their clothing like this at home, things would be a lot less chaotic," Tessa said, hanging the last dress on a mobile rack while Izzy and Ashley placed the accessories into cubbies along the wall. Tessa's daughters seemed to be getting along for a change. They'd focused on their mutual dislike for Austin Greer. I could hear them grumbling—likely plotting his demise—as they finished their tasks.

"Do you think we need to lock up Frankie's jewelry?" I asked Tessa, eyeing the open cubbies at the back of the room. I thought it was probably a bit too expensive to leave out overnight. "I'll go ask Frankie."

I couldn't find Frankie onstage or in what he'd called the house, so I headed for the lobby. As I passed through the seating area, I noticed a tattooed woman with a shaved head sitting by herself in the back row of the theater. While I would never choose to shave my head, I'd ended up with extremely short bangs last year after I got too close to a hot kiln and singed them off. Since then I'd been wearing my light brown hair in a short pixie cut.

I was pretty sure this woman's hair—or lack of it—was a fashion statement, rather than an accident as mine had been. As Val would say, it worked for her. I wasn't sure who it was, but if I had to put money on it, I'd say it was Vega. I'd seen pictures of her in one of the glass art magazines I subscribed to. Tessa, who knew nearly everyone in Seattle's glass scene, told me Vega liked pushing boundaries in her artwork. While she was well-regarded, she was not well liked. Apparently, she was one of the only glassblowers who blew glass without a partner. As I had learned a few weeks ago, glassblowing with a partner was extremely difficult. I imagined it would be nearly impossible without one. Of course, for me, glassblowing was nearly impossible in general, except when my life—or Tessa's—depended on it.

I spotted Frankie and Mr. Greer in the lobby arguing with a man I'd not seen before. I made a quick retreat back to the dressing room since they didn't look they were having a friendly, or interruptible, conversation.

"I'm going to have to talk with Frankie later," I said to Tessa. "He seems to be involved in a heated discussion with Austin and another man I don't know." Just to be safe, we gathered the jewelry into trays, slid them into the storage cubbies, and covered them with some scarves to keep them out of sight.

"Oh, I bet that's Daniel Owens. He's the manager here at the theater," Tessa said as she corralled a few belts into a box and tucked it beneath the clothing rack.

Once we finished our duties and made sure all the girls had been picked up by their parents, Tessa and I left with her daughters. Since she had parked her minivan on the street near the front of the theater, we went through the lobby. Austin, Frankie, and Daniel were still arguing and had been joined by a woman with short black hair who was hurling epithets at all three men. As we silently passed them, I realized we were in for more drama than we'd bargained for at the theater.

TWO

TESSA'S VAN, as usual, was trashed inside, full of the detritus that comes from having three active kids and a schedule a little too full to take care of tasks like cleaning out your car. Izzy and Ashley spent the trip home complaining about Mr. Greer. Since they were speaking in whispers in the backseat, I only caught a few snatches of their conversation, like "so unfair," "sucks," and "like, totally mean."

As Tessa drove me home, I got a call on my cell phone.

"Hello, Jax? This is Nika Petrovich. We met earlier today. I've spoken with Mrs. Greer, and she'd very much like you to come see her on Friday." Nika and I made plans for my visit, and I hung up the phone.

Tessa glanced my way. "What was that all about?"

"Amanda Greer is interested in looking at my beads and jewelry."

"Congratulations. That's fantastic. I hope she buys a lot from you," Tessa said as she turned down the long alley next to my house and parked.

"I hope so, too. From the sounds of it, she has money to spend." I waved goodbye as Tessa made a six-point turn behind my house and headed home to her husband, Craig, and their youngest child—little Joey, a surprise addition to their family twelve years after Ashley was born.

I crossed the patio and let myself in through the back door. Coming into my studio, I found my fat, gray cat, Gumdrop, snoozing in his favorite spot, my worktable. Dropping my handbag on the table, I gave Gummie some head scratches, then walked down the hall to the kitchen. My Craftsman-style duplex, which I'd inherited from Great-Aunt Rita, was slowly coming together after a couple of years of renovations.

I was starving after all the work I'd done at the theater, so I made a grilled cheese sandwich and ate it while sitting in front of the laptop in my office-cum-guest room. The Bead Lair, as Tessa had nicknamed this room, was a cozy little spot where I stored my extra beads. In addition to a desk I used for doing paperwork, there was a daybed guests could use when they came to visit. Tonight it was not the Bead Lair, but the Bill Lair, as I grappled with the stack of bills that had arrived a week ago, which I had been putting off paying. I winced as I opened each envelope, and only once because of a paper cut. When I was done, my bank account was nearly empty. Although Aunt Rita had given me this house and a hefty bankroll when she passed away, I didn't like dipping into that nest egg. Instead, I was trying my best to live on what I made as a glass beadmaker.

Now that I was a glass artist, I was happier than I'd ever been. It was a choice I'd made three years ago when I left Miami and my useless boyfriend, Jerry, behind. He'd started to love booze and televised sports more than he loved me. Leaving my home in Florida behind had been difficult, but the friendships I had made here in Seattle had grown strong in the last few years. While I did feel homesick from time to time, this was the place I belonged, along with my catnip-addicted feline friend.

It was late when I finished the bills, but I wasn't ready to go to bed. I was tempted to fill a jumbo-sized wine glass and drink away my worries. While that would have been in my ex-boyfriend's playbook, it wasn't in mine. I needed to clean out my attic, which was the very last thing I wanted to do. My attic was spooky. I'd only been up there a couple of times, and I'd always spent as little time as possible in it. I had an aversion to small, spider-infested spaces. A spider web streaking across my face could make me want to pee my pants, or at least bolt out the door.

Tessa had remodeled her attic during spring break, and it turned out so well I decided I should do it too. My project would be much smaller, because I didn't have as much to spend, and because my attic was tiny compared to hers. Part of my motivation to complete the project sooner rather than later was that my sister Connie's son, Jeremy, was coming to visit. He had painted many of the watercolors that brightened my home and was a talented young artist. I had promised him he could stay with me this summer while he was taking an art class at the University of Washington. It would only be another month before Jeremy arrived, so I had to stop procrastinating and get to work on my attic so my nephew could have the Bead Lair, and I would have my new attic space to use as an office.

Rudy, a painting contractor, was one of Val's makeover clients—some would say victims—whom she'd met last spring. They'd become fast friends since they were both obsessed with science fiction movies. I'd often find Rudy in Val's half of the duplex watching Star Wars movies. He had worked on Tessa's attic remodel and said he would help with my project, too. When he visited last week he broke the news to me that my attic needed more than painting, but that he could handle the additional work. As long as I helped with some of the labor, he could do the project during his spare time and would work for the cost of materials, plus some glass beads. Anytime I could trade beads for something I couldn't do on my own, I was happy with the arrangement.

Remembering how my cat had caused so much trouble the last time I'd opened the attic, I grabbed Gumdrop and tossed him into the hallway, then shut the door to my studio. I wasn't going to chase him around my attic through the dust and spider webs as I'd had to do last time I ventured in. With Gumdrop safely locked out, I grabbed the flashlight I kept at the back door, then headed up the stairs, careful to step around all the boxes of beads I had stacked there.

After switching on the flashlight, I let the light play across the rough pine floorboards. Fortunately, there wasn't much up here other than a few boxes, a brass floor lamp that had seen better days, a ghostly-looking chair covered in a sheet, decades of dust, and the inevitable webs between the bare wall studs. I couldn't wait until all the nooks and crannies were covered with drywall and a fresh coat of paint and all the hiding places for creepy-crawlies were eliminated. As I looked around the room, I noticed a bare bulb dangling from the ceiling. I pulled on the cord at the base of the fixture to try the light. Nothing. I ran downstairs, grabbed a bulb, returned to the attic, and swapped out the old one in the simple fixture. Light flooded the room. Up until this moment, I hadn't had high hopes for what this space would look like. Looking around now, though, I could tell it was going to be terrific when it was complete.

Grabbing the old floor lamp, I pulled it out the door, and dragged it downstairs. Then I tossed its moth-eaten shade in the trashcan and carried the rest of the lamp to my car. I would take it to Goodwill when I had a chance. Heading back into the attic, I tried to tackle the ghostly-looking chair, but it was too heavy to budge. Rudy was going to have to move that himself.

The next step was to get a broom and knock down the cobwebs, but I couldn't bring myself to do it. Where there were webs, there were spiders. I wasn't in the mood to tackle any eight-legged creatures tonight, or any night for that matter.

At midnight I crawled into bed with Gumdrop, who was curled up on my pillow. He often complained about it, but I refused to share a pillow with him. I moved him to the blanket at the foot of the bed, and we both fell fast asleep.

THREE

TESSA WAS AT MY DOOR bright and early the next morning, juggling two coffees and a bakery bag as she opened the door and let herself in.

"Rise and shine, sleepyhead!" she said. I shuffled out of my bedroom and down the hall toward the kitchen, where she stood arranging the breakfast items on the round oak table.

"You are my very best friend," I said, hugging her.

"Thanks, and you are mine."

"Can you tell me one thing?"

"Sure."

"Why are you here so early? Austin Greer told us we didn't have to be at the theater until four o'clock."

"Yes, that's true, if we were only working on the fashion show," Tessa said.

"I thought that's what we were doing." I took a cup of coffee out of the cardboard tray.

"I also volunteered us for the auction—all part of the fundraiser for the Homeless Advocacy Team."

I closed my eyes tight and tried not to react. Tessa had a lot of energy, especially early in the morning. I honestly didn't know how she could have that much stamina with three kids, a retail shop, a glass studio, a husband, and a house.

"Aah..." I said, figuring this was my safest response.

"And so we need to get to the theater early to meet with the fundraising coordinator, Jaya Bakshi."

"Aah..."

"So we need to get going."

"Aah—"

"Don't say 'aah' again, or else I'm going to leave and take your breakfast with me."

"You'd take my coffee?" I asked, clutching it protectively against my chest, much like Mr. Greer had done yesterday when I bumped into him.

"I don't think I could get you to part with that coffee." She grabbed the white bakery bag from the table and dangled it in front of me. "But I could probably run faster than you. I have chocolate chip muffins that I'm going to hold hostage until you're ready to go."

"You wouldn't!"

"I would. Now go! Get ready, or I'm going to have to eat both of these delicious muffins."

"You win. I'm going," I said, knowing I was defeated. Plus, I'd do almost anything, provided it was legal, for a chocolate chip muffin. I headed back to my bedroom to get dressed while Tessa sat down at the table to have her breakfast. "There better be a muffin left for me when I get back."

Tessa took a bite of the muffin. "You better hurry. These are delicious."

I got ready in minutes and joined Tessa at the table. She was right—they were some pretty amazing muffins

• • •

It's never a positive sign to show up somewhere and discover four police cars in the parking lot with their lights flashing, but that's what we saw when we pulled up at the Chanticleer Theater.

I parked the Ladybug, my lovely red convertible VW bug, in the parking lot behind the theater, well away from the commotion at the backstage door. Tessa and I made our way to the door, where two burly police officers who were blocking the entrance stopped us.

"Sorry, ladies," the shorter of the two officers said. "We've had an incident, and we are not allowing access to the theater at this time."

"What kind of incident?" Tessa asked.

I grabbed Tessa by the hand and pulled her away.

"See that white van over there?" I whispered. "You know what that is, right?"

"Ambulance?"

"Try again," I said.

"Ice cream truck?" Tessa said with a smirk. "I don't know, Jax—oh…" It finally hit Tessa. That was a medical examiner's van. In my experience, a coroner's vehicle parked outside a building could mean only one thing. Someone had died.

Two men in disposable white coveralls rolled a gurney with a blue body bag on it out the backstage door of the theater. Without a word, they slid the body bag and stretcher into the van and drove away. We returned to the police officers.

"Can you at least tell us who was wheeled out of here?" I asked the officers. Just then, Daniel Owens appeared in the doorway, looking disheveled and confused.

"Hi, Daniel—we haven't met, I'm Jax, one of the volunteers for the Homeless Advocacy Team fashion show—"

"And auction," Tessa added.

"We were wondering —what happened? Is everything okay?" I asked, although I knew from the body bag that it wasn't.

"No, everything is not okay. I found Austin Greer, and he was—was—" The man crumpled into Tessa's arms.

Tessa, a mom through-and-through, held Daniel and patted him on the back reassuringly.

"Oh, no. Austin, dead? I can't believe it. I'm so sorry," I said. "How can we help you?"

"I just want to forget what I saw, I—" Daniel released his grip on

Tessa and ran his hands through his thinning hair. "Sorry…"

"You know what? I need a cup of coffee. How about you, Tessa?"

"No, I'm good," she said, oblivious to where I was headed with my suggestion.

"Oh, no, I don't think you are." I gave her one of those wide-eyed read-my-mind looks Gumdrop sometimes gives me. His stares are usually a request for catnip, so his mind isn't that hard to read. I thought if we could get Daniel away from the theater for a cup of coffee, we might learn a little bit more about what had happened, and comfort him at the same time. Plus, I felt I could use another caffeine fix.

"Come to think of it, I do need some coffee," Tessa said, finally catching on. "Come on, Daniel. I'll buy you a cup."

"On second thought, those officers may not want you to go," I said as I glanced over at the police officers who were watching us.

"They said it was okay if I leave," Daniel said. "I gave them my phone number and address, and I told them what I saw. I'm pretty sure they'll want to talk to me again." Daniel reminded me of a young Woody Allen, pale, weak, neurotic—like he needed to spend a little more time outdoors and little less time in the dark passageways of an old theater.

We walked to the Starbucks across the square. While I ordered us all Venti coffees, Tessa snagged a grouping of comfortable leather armchairs. I brought over the coffee, along with sugar and stir sticks, and set them down on a metal table between the chairs.

After a few sips of coffee, Daniel started to relax and open up.

"Austin. He helped all those kids, you know. He helped me personally on so many things. And to see him there, crushed…"

"Crushed?" I had visions of a pillar from a faux new-wave castle falling over on the poor man.

"And everyone at the Homeless Advocacy Team is going to be crushed, too," Daniel said, after taking a large swallow of coffee.

"Of course, everyone will be crushed to hear of Austin's death," Tessa said.

"No, the chandelier—it's crushed. All that money HAT could

have raised, shattered into a million pieces all over the stage." Daniel sucked in a shuddering breath.

Tessa and I were starting to put things together. I didn't want to be the one to say the horrifying truth out loud: Austin Greer had been crushed by the Vega chandelier. The sheer thought of it made me shiver. What a horrible way to die—and what an awful thing to have seen, even after the fact. No wonder Daniel was so shaken. Tessa and I had seen a couple of dead bodies, and I could honestly say I never wanted to see another one. This death seemed particularly gruesome, and I tried not to think of how horrible it must have been.

"Well, accidents happen," Tessa said. "It sounds like maybe the chandelier was installed incorrectly. Certainly, you have more to worry about than the fact that the Homeless Advocacy Team won't have the chandelier to auction off," Tessa said. And she was right, there was more to worry about than the chandelier. I had to wonder, though, if this really had been an accident. It certainly seemed strange the chandelier would fall at all—and awfully convenient that it had fallen on someone. If the cables that held the chandelier in place had failed, what were the chances it would hit someone? I decided to keep this theory to myself, and not risk upsetting Daniel further.

"Tessa's right. You've had a big shock, and you need to take care of yourself. I'm sure HAT will find another way to raise the money they need," I said, finishing the last of my coffee.

"With Austin gone, I'm all that theater has left. I can't stop now. I've just got to keep going."

While I approved of Daniel's work ethic, I worried he'd have a nervous breakdown if he couldn't pull himself together.

"And—who's going to clean up that mess? I don't want to have to deal with all the blood and broken glass," Daniel said. This seemed like a strange thing for Daniel to fret about, but he must have been worried it would end up being him. Sometimes people who are in shock can think of the strangest things. He seemed to be the only one who worked at the theater on a full-time basis, especially now that Austin was no longer among the living.

"There are companies you can hire to clean up messes after something like this happens," Tessa offered, always practical.

"We're rehearsing a show—you must know *Hamlet* opens next week. Even with Austin gone, we've got to keep going. As we say in the theater, the show must go on!"

"Right. And we're hoping we'll still be able to have our gala, too," Tessa said.

"We'll just have to see how long the police need to investigate. The theater will probably be shut down for a day or two," I said.

"A day or two? With Austin gone, there's no reason for Amanda to keep the theater running. She could shut us down permanently! Oh, my God, I hadn't thought of that. I could lose my job, I could—" Daniel was starting to tear up again. Tessa pulled a tissue from her purse and handed it to him. He blotted his eyes and blew his nose, then stuffed the tissue in the top of his empty cup.

Poor Daniel was a wreck, but he did have a point. The future of the theater was in jeopardy. With Austin gone, who knew whether Austin's wife would be interested in continuing with her support of the theater? I was sure she'd be devastated by the loss of her husband, and it would be up to her to decide what to do with the theater.

"Don't worry," I said. "We have to carry on without Austin. That's all we can do. I'm sure everything will work out fine."

I had no way of knowing it was already too late for that.

FOUR

TESSA AND I WALKED BACK from the coffee shop with Daniel. He seemed to have gotten a little steadier on his feet.

"So, what now?" Tessa asked when we arrived back at the parking lot behind the Chanticleer Theater.

"I'm going to stay here and wait until the police are gone and then maybe I can get backstage and get some work done," Daniel said, his eyes widening as he watched two uniformed officers tote plastic bins out the backstage door. "Excuse me—what are you removing? You have no right to take that stuff!" He rushed toward one of the officers to look inside a bin.

"Evidence," one of the officers replied, tapping on the lid of the tub with his free hand.

"What kind of evidence? We've got a show to do. You better not be taking any of the props!" Daniel replied.

"I don't think you'll be needing this. It's just a bunch of glass bits," the officer said.

My heart sank. They were carrying away the chandelier, all one million pieces of it. Another officer exited the building, pushing a cart loaded with a mangled lighting fixture. It didn't look like it was part of the destroyed chandelier.

"Oh, no—you can't take the ghost light. Every theater has to have a ghost light," said Daniel, rushing toward the cart to try and grab the fixture. The officer held up a warning hand to keep Daniel back.

"Sorry, sir, just following orders from the homicide division." The words "homicide division" made me wince. It was likely those orders had come from my boyfriend, Zachary Grant, who was a detective working for the Seattle Police Department. If he wasn't here now, he had been. I didn't dare ask the officer if Zachary was here for fear it would get back to him. It also meant Mr. Greer's death had not been an accident, as I had surmised.

"I'm sure you can do without one for a little while," I said. It had been a floor lamp on wheels—nothing special, and now it was just a pile of crushed metal tubing and wires. I couldn't understand why Daniel was having such a conniption about it.

"No! You obviously know nothing about show business. Every theater must have a ghost light."

"Why?" Tessa and I asked at the same time. It was likely something obvious, but we simply didn't know.

"It's a theater tradition—a superstition. You leave a light on in the middle of the stage when the theater isn't occupied. Every theater I've ever worked in has had a ghost light—every theater everywhere has one."

"Do all theaters have ghosts?" Tessa asked. Tessa and I had thought we'd encountered a ghost in an elevator last fall while we were attending a bead bazaar in Portland, Oregon. It turned out it wasn't a haunting, but something far more mundane that had caused the creepy coldness in the elevator at the Red Rose Hotel. Turning to me, she added, "It's fortunate Val isn't here. She'd be spraying her perfume everywhere." That was true. Val, who most definitely believed in spirits, thought perfume was a cure for the common ghost.

"Some theaters do have ghosts, I suppose. But you know, the ghost light does more than keep ghosts away. It also prevents people from walking around in the dark and falling into the orchestra pit," Daniel said. He had a good point—for safety's sake, having a light on stage could prevent any number of accidents from happening in the dark. It was like having a giant nightlight.

"Maybe I can help. I have an old floor lamp in the back seat of my car. I was heading over to Goodwill to donate it, but if you'd like it, it's yours, at least until you can get one you like better," I said. I was happy to give it to him. It would save me a trip to the donation center.

"Yes, please. I think now more than ever, we need the light. With Austin dying on the stage, we probably have a real ghost now, if we didn't have one before."

I retrieved the light from the Ladybug and handed it over to Daniel. "It needs a bulb, but other than that it should work fine," I said.

"Thank you," Daniel said, examining the light and nodding weakly.

He approached the police officers by the backstage door who had been unwilling to let us in earlier. After a few minutes of talking and gesticulation, Daniel gave up trying to convince them to let him back in and carried the light through the parking lot and around to the front of the building. The officers must have decided Daniel could enter the building, but not through the backstage door. I assumed this meant Daniel could work in the theater's box office, but he wouldn't be allowed onto the stage until the detectives and CSI personnel had completed their work.

A blue Toyota sedan parked in a space nearby. The driver, a thirty-something woman in leggings and an oversized sweater, got out of the car. She saw us and headed our way.

"Jaya Bakshi. I'm from the Homeless Advocacy Team." She extended her hand to us. We each shook it and introduced ourselves to her. "I'm here for the auction meeting. What's going on over there?" She asked, nodding toward the police cars.

Apparently, she hadn't yet heard about Austin's demise.

Tessa broke the news to her as gently as possible.

"Oh, how devastating! So sad, of course, for Austin's family, but it's a sad day for HAT, as well. Mr. Greer was such an important donor and friend. I'll have to talk with the board of directors to determine what they want to do. The board will want to go ahead and auction off the chandelier, at least." Jaya shook her head as if to clear her mind of negative thoughts.

Tessa broke the news to Jaya about the demolished chandelier.

"Oh, no! That's terrible. We were relying on those funds to keep our doors open. Without it, I don't know what we'll do," Jaya said, trying to remain composed. "I guess we'll just have to find another way to raise the money."

"Don't worry. We're going to make sure the event happens. We'll raise that money, maybe not as much as we would have with the chandelier, but we'll do our best," Tessa said.

I nodded in agreement.

"Thank you, both. Really. The Homeless Advocacy Team has several worthwhile programs that are helping a lot of teens and young adults, but we can't do it without funding, of course. I'll talk with the board and let them know you're willing to continue with the gala, and I expect they'll agree to carry on. I've already sent out announcements to our current donor list about the auction. So, if you can somehow still make this event happen, I'll make sure we have people to fill the seats."

"We'll do our best," Tessa said.

"Now, I need to get inside and talk with Daniel. Thank you so very much for your support. Please call the HAT offices if you need anything," Jaya said as she made a beeline for the backstage door.

"You'll need to go through the front door, the officers aren't letting anyone in through the backstage," Tessa called out to her.

Jaya waved and nodded as she adjusted her course and headed for the front of the theater as Daniel had done a few minutes before.

With nothing else to do at the theater, Tessa and I drove back to my house. We needed to call the volunteers and let them know what had happened and that rehearsals were canceled, at least for today.

I had made plans to go out with Zachary that evening. We'd been dating since Valentine's Day, and things had started to get pretty serious, although in general, he was far more serious about most things than I was. He was stern yet sexy, in just the right proportions.

When he took off his glasses and looked at me, he could melt my heart.

Zachary called me as I unlocked my door and stepped into the studio.

"Hi, how's it going?" I asked.

"Not so good. I'm sorry, but we can't get together tonight," Zachary said. I heard a tightness in his voice. The last time I'd heard it, I was mixed up in a homicide investigation he was working on.

"What happened? A murder?"

"I can't talk about it."

"Can't or won't?"

Silence.

"Where are you headed? Maybe I could tag along," I said.

"No, that would be inadvisable," he said, the sternness in his voice escalating.

"Maybe I can guess. You're headed to the Chanticleer Theater—"

"How could you possibly know that?"

"Aha! So you are heading to the Chanticleer Theater."

"I didn't say that," he said, exasperated.

"But you are, right? Tessa and I were there earlier today."

"You always know how to be in the wrong place at the wrong time. I suppose someone interviewed you?"

"Nope. The officers wouldn't let us into the theater and didn't want to talk with us."

Zachary was silent, a sure sign he was perturbed with me—or with someone on his team who should have gotten my name and contact information.

"Jax, this is a likely homicide. The Crime Scene Investigation techs have already determined that someone disengaged the safety chain on the chandelier, and the cord that held the chandelier in place had been cut."

"Not an accident?"

"No way. That's why I've been called in."

"I could help you, you know," I offered.

"Sorry, Jax. I'd rather not mix my professional life with my personal life."

"I'm part of your personal life. That's good news."

"You are. And I don't want you to get hurt."

"Right, me neither, but you can't really control that…"

"I'll call you tomorrow." And then the line went dead. It felt a little like he'd hung up on me. It was possible his phone had died, or he'd entered an area with poor cell coverage. Or, he'd hung up on me. I didn't want to consider that last option.

I spent the evening making glass beads. It's my job, but it's also my passion. Lighting my torch, melting glass, and shaping it into beads had always been therapeutic for me. As I sat at my torch, I felt a calm settle over me that I often experienced when I worked creatively. I was making a bead with an ocean motif, complete with a sandy shore and turquoise waves. It felt like playtime to me and was helping me forget the horrible things that had happened today. I'd recently put a bumper sticker on my car that said *Plays with Fire*, and that was exactly what I was doing—pouring my creative energy into working with glass to take my mind off Zachary and forget about the death of Austin Greer. After working on the torch for a few hours and stuffing my kiln with a dozen new glass beads, I started the annealing program on the kiln so the beads would cool down slowly overnight.

Around dinnertime, I wandered out to my kitchen and rummaged through the refrigerator looking for something to eat. I wondered if Val, who lived in the other half of the duplex, might be home and have something for dinner that would be better than the leftover sourdough bread and spray-can cheese I was contemplating. I admit I let Val take care of me, just a little bit. She advised me about making appropriate fashion choices, and she cooked for me now and then, among other things.

Val's cooking skills were inconsistent at best. She tended to use a little too much of everything in her recipes. Sometimes this worked to her advantage. Extra cheese and extra chocolate—those didn't seem to take her down a disastrous path. However, additional chili powder, baking powder, or herbs had rendered many potentially delicious meals inedible.

I opened the front door and nearly slammed into Val.

"Hello, sweet cheeks!" Val said, her faux-leopard clad arms cradling an oval tureen of soup. "I was hoping you would be home. I have a lot of this soup, and tomorrow's a full moon, so I've got to get it out of my house before I eat it."

"What? Why?" I asked as Val barged past me and placed the bowl on my kitchen table.

"Didn't I tell you? I'm on the Werewolf Diet! I'm a teensy-weensy too voluptuous for my Princess Leia costume. I refuse to wear Spanx, so I'm going to drop a couple of quick pounds." This was news to me. Val had never once mentioned the word "diet" to me, but it certainly wasn't the first time she'd mentioned werewolves.

"Werewolf Diet? Sounds drastic. Do you have to get bitten by a werewolf to be on the diet? Because if you do it may take some time to find one in Seattle. If you go out to Forks on the Olympic Peninsula, you'd likely find some werewolves."

"I've got news for you, darling, Twilight is fiction, so we won't find any werewolves out there. But see, this diet, it's all about the phase of the moon. When there's a full moon, I can only drink clear liquids, and that's tomorrow. So, I have to remove all the tempting food from my house. I sent all the cookies home with Rudy."

Dammit. I would have taken those cookies off her hands, no problem.

"Thanks for the soup. It looks yummy." I grabbed a ladle, spoons, and bowls from the kitchen and brought them to the table.

"It's cream of potato," she said, ladling the soup into the bowls.

I sampled the soup. Holy moly! I'd never tasted so much garlic in my life.

"Wow! There's a lot of garlic in this," I said as I choked a little.

"I added a few extra cloves because I adore garlic. Since I don't have a boyfriend right now, I don't have to worry about kissing anyone with stinky breath. Oh—but maybe you shouldn't have too much if you going out with Zachary tonight."

"Nope. He called to say he was busy with an investigation. It wasn't one of our better conversations."

"I'm sorry sweetums, you know he's not always the best communicator when he's stressed, and neither are you. I'm sure you two will work it out."

Sweat beaded on my forehead as I ate a few more spoonfuls. I wasn't sure I'd be able to finish the bowl. I grabbed the sourdough from the counter and cut a slice for each of us. "Here you go, this will be nice with the soup." I hoped the bread would counteract the garlic.

"Um, Val? You know with all this garlic, I'm not sure you're going to find a single werewolf to hang out with tomorrow," I said, teasing her.

"Oh, but you're wrong!" Val shook her head from side to side, as her red curls bounced right along with her.

"I'm wrong about the werewolves? You're actually going to hang out with some tomorrow during the full moon?"

"Werewolves don't care about garlic. It's vampires who don't like garlic! What I've heard is that werewolves love garlic because it makes their coat nice and shiny."

I decided it was time to move on. When Val got going on her strange topics, she could go on for hours.

"You said you're boyfriend-free right now? What happened to the massage therapist?"

"He's been gone for ages. He only wanted to give me massages."

"Sounds fantastic to me," I replied, cutting more bread for us.

"You know, he wasn't my type. I need someone a little more... alive! He was on the mellow end of the spectrum. But it's okay. I've got you and Gumdrop, and I've got Stanley, too." Stanley was Val's basset hound, who she adopted after his owner went to jail.

"You most certainly do," I said, as I continued to eat the soup, feeling like the odor of garlic was going to ooze from my pores for days to come. "Thanks for bringing over dinner. I've had a rough day."

"Why, sugarplum? What happened?"

"Tessa and I are volunteering at the Chanticleer Theater next to

Yesler Square. The owner turned up dead this morning. It was awful. Poor guy was killed by a chandelier."

"Well, that doesn't make much sense," Val said, sipping the last drop of soup from her spoon.

"It does when the chandelier falls and squashes him—and cuts him to ribbons, I assume, because the fixture was made of glass."

"Ugh! If I hadn't just eaten, that would have made me lose my appetite," Val said, as she carried her bowl to the sink. "Well, you just let the police handle it, okay?"

"You sound like Zachary. He told me the same thing. I promised not to meddle in the investigation."

"Well, darling, don't you fret. It will all work out, I'm sure." Val sashayed out the door, taking her soup tureen and her toxic soup with her.

After cleaning up the kitchen, I went in search of Gumdrop. I hadn't seen him all evening. That was odd, because usually when anyone was in the kitchen Gummie came running to see if there were any treats for him. My cat often made himself invisible when Val brought Stanley the basset hound over, but tonight he hadn't come with her. I wondered if I'd find Val and Stanley on the front porch tomorrow night howling at the full moon. It wouldn't surprise me if they did, and it wouldn't really bother me, either. Heck, I might even join them.

I found Gumdrop asleep on a big pile of beads on the worktable near the window by the back door of my studio. "Come on," I said, picking up my fluffy, gray cat. I heard a rumble over the sound of beads rolling off the table and hitting the floor. It wasn't a purr; it was a growl. Gummie looked up and glared at me with his big green eyes. He was unhappy and didn't want to be moved. Carefully, I set him down on the workbench. I grabbed an old towel from a drawer and laid it out on the counter. Then I gently scooted him onto his makeshift bed, hoping he wouldn't growl at me again.

"All right, you big baby, now you can at least be comfortable." I felt a slight breeze, and, realizing the window was open a smidge, reached under the blinds to close it. "There. Now you won't get chilled," I told my cat.

Tessa called as I was getting ready for bed. She told me Daniel had called her to say we'd be allowed back into the Chanticleer in the morning, but that we'd have to work in the rehearsal space and not on the stage. We made a plan to meet there tomorrow, first thing.

I climbed into bed, pulling one of my Great-Aunt Rita's beautiful handmade quilts around me. I was glad to be here—in this bed, in this cozy house. As I fell asleep, I couldn't help thinking about Mr. Greer—his death wasn't an accident. I wondered if it was safe for us to be in the theater. Who could have killed Austin Greer and what motive would they have had? And while I agreed with Daniel that the show must go on, I wondered if it was worth the risk of being there. After all, a murderer had been in the Chanticleer Theater, and might still be there, ready to strike again.

FIVE

THE FOLLOWING MORNING I went to the Chanticleer Theater to meet Tessa, as we'd agreed. Unsure whether the police would allow us in through the backstage door today, I decided to park on the street near the front entrance. As I walked to the theater, I passed a high-end clothing shop on the corner of Yesler Square. The proprietor of the boutique stood on the sidewalk, supervising a worker who was installing collapsible security gates across the front of the full-length windows outside.

I stopped and looked in the windows. This was the kind of shop I loved, full of interesting clothing in unusual colors. The fabrics looked soft and the styles unfussy and unstructured—in other words, they looked comfy, yet elegant. What really stood out to me was that the store didn't seem to have any jewelry for sale. As I stared at the store's displays, I tried to figure out what kind of jewelry I would coordinate with these clothes. The owner, an impeccably-dressed woman about my age with an interesting asymmetrical haircut, made eye contact with me and smiled.

"Excuse the chaos out here. Please come in," the woman said, pushing the door open and inviting me into her store.

"Sorry if I seemed to have been a bit spaced out. I was thinking about what kind of jewelry I'd wear with some of these outfits. Plus, I think I'm in desperate need of another cup of coffee," I said, admiring a pair of cropped black pants and a fiery red tunic with a lovely drape to it.

"Yes, it's unusual that I don't have any jewelry right now. Unfortunately, I'm between designers—the last one didn't work out."

"Do you have someone else lined up? If not, we both may be in luck. I make my own glass beads and jewelry. Like this." I removed the necklace I had on. It was one of my favorites, featuring a set of blue and white swirled glass orbs, strung together on silk cord.

"Oh, I love this! It would work well with several outfits I have right now." The woman held the necklace up to the denim shirtdress she was wearing. Looking in the mirror, she nodded her approval before handing it back to me.

"I'd be happy to bring some samples by," I said as I rummaged through my handbag looking for a business card. Finally, I found my card and handed it to her. "I'm Jax O'Connell. Here's my contact information. I've got a website, too, so you can see images of my work."

"Thanks, and I'm Cassie Morton. I'll check out your work online, and I look forward to seeing your work in person. And please, feel free to shop today." She pressed her business card into my hand, and I tucked it into my purse.

"I'd love to shop, but I need to stop by another day," I said, heading for the door. "I've got to get over to the theater."

"The theater? Is there something going on over there?"

"Oh, we've been rehearsing for an upcoming fashion show and benefit auction."

"No, I saw a lot of cop cars over there yesterday."

"The owner of the theater passed away."

"What timing," Cassie muttered.

"Excuse me? Did you know Mr. Greer well?"

"Oh, nothing. I wish I could say I'll miss Austin, but he was a bit of a thorn in my side."

"I'm sorry to hear that. I didn't really know him." I decided not to add that several other people felt the same way or that it appeared Mr. Greer had died under suspicious circumstances.

"I promise I'll come back and shop again soon," I said, as I left the boutique.

• • •

I passed through the theater lobby and into the house. It was quiet and dark onstage. This was where Austin Greer had died less than two days before. Shivers ran down my spine as I looked up to the spot on the ceiling where Vega's glass chandelier had once hung. I swallowed hard and wished we'd never committed to continuing with the gala in light of what had happened here. Apparently, Daniel hadn't started using his new ghost light yet, so I could only faintly make out the dim outline of the castle set pieces. As I walked by the rows of seats, I spotted Tessa standing near a side door at the bottom of the steps that led from the stage to the seats.

"This way—the police won't let us use the stage today, so we have to use the rehearsal space downstairs," Tessa said.

Inside the door were more steps leading down. I followed her down the staircase. While it had been eerily calm upstairs, it was a completely different story in the basement. Daniel was standing in the middle of the room trying—and failing—to get everyone's attention. Tessa spotted the red bullhorn Frankie had been using the day before yesterday and grabbed it. Daniel, relieved of the challenge of bringing order to a group of teenage girls, slipped out the door at his first opportunity. I'm sure he had better things to do, and come to think of it, so did I, but Tessa would never forgive me if I bailed out on her now.

"Everyone! Listen to me!" Tessa was bossy enough that everyone immediately stopped what they were doing as a hush fell over the room. "I'd like everyone to gather here with me in a circle. Now, first off, you've all heard of the terrible accident with Austin here at the theater. Now, without him, we're all going to have to work extra hard to pull off this event," Tessa told the gathered crowd. "I want everyone to please be careful. The theater is a dangerous place, and accidents can happen."

I didn't correct her. I knew Austin's death wasn't an accident, but I didn't want her or anyone else to panic.

Frankie stood at the edge of the group, looking sullen and fretful. While Tessa continued her pep talk, I approached him.

"This is the worst," Frankie said with a grimace.

"I know, it's horrible, but I think we have to carry on," I replied.

"Tessa didn't tell me I was going to be working with Austin Greer in the first place. Now he turns up dead. I can't believe I ever said yes to doing this. I thought it might help me get some exposure and increase sales at my gallery."

"It's going to be fine," I said, trying to soothe Frankie. He was turning out to be quite a diva. He belonged in the theater.

"Look—I don't feel safe here. This whole thing is a disaster," he said. "I should never have agreed to do this."

"But we are so glad you did. We really need you," I said, patting Frankie's shoulder encouragingly. I knew how he felt. Being in this theater, where Mr. Greer had died so violently, had given me the jitters, as well. But I had to wonder, was it theaters in general that worried Frankie, or was he concerned, perhaps, that the falling chandelier was meant for him, or was it something else entirely that was bothering him?

"I don't want to be the next one they're taking to the morgue. Besides, I don't think this is going to be the best thing for my brand at this point," Frankie said, brushing my hand away.

"You're not quitting, are you?" I stood up as tall as possible to try and look fierce. I didn't think it was working.

"I can't believe you're going to try and continue. You two can't run this thing. And I'm certainly not going to take it over—I've got far too much to do. I suggest you take my lead and shut this whole thing down.

"We can't do that. Think of all the people the money from this event will help. Think of the volunteers—"

"I'll make a donation. You should do the same, then you can go back to your studio and make some beads—you're better at that anyway."

"Frankie, you can't go. We need you." My voice was getting a little loud for this confined space, but I was just about to lose my temper.

"I'm leaving." He was done, and there appeared to be no way to stop him.

"Fine! You want to leave? Just go." I'd lost my patience with this man. If he wanted to go, then good riddance.

Frankie arched both of his well-groomed eyebrows in astonishment, turned, and headed up the stairs. Tessa saw him leave and broke away from her pep talk with the girls to ask me what was going on. I filled her in.

"I'm sorry. I lost my cool," I said.

Tessa took off up the stairs in search of Frankie.

"Wait! Frankie. Don't go. We need you!" Tessa shouted, in hot pursuit. I followed along behind her, making apologetic sounds as we huffed up the stairs.

Frankie stopped and turned around at the top of the steps, panting. "Your friend Jax doesn't seem to agree. I refuse to stay where I'm not appreciated." Frankie took a left at the top of the stairs and went into the dressing room. Tessa and I were hot on his heels. He grabbed his necklaces from the trays in the storage bins, jammed them into his leather satchel, and barged past us on his way to the lobby.

"Wait! Frankie! You can't take your jewelry! We need it for the event," I shouted after him. But it was too late. He was gone, chugging out the door on feet that were too small for his broad frame.

"Ugh! What are we going to do now?" I asked Tessa.

She dropped onto a shabby loveseat in the dressing room.

I sat down next to her. "We can't quit, can we?"

"No, of course not. We already told Jaya we'd raise the money for HAT. Think of all the homeless teens HAT can help, plus the girls will be so disappointed if we cancel."

"Looks like we're going to need to find another emcee—preferably someone famous," I said, knowing Tessa, as usual, was right. Quitting was for losers. We might not have known what in the heck we were doing, but we were definitely not losers. "Maybe I can ask Val if her Uncle Freddie is available." Val's uncle, Freddie "Boom Boom" Roberts, was an aging rock superstar who had recently moved to the area. Since he seemed to like me, I might be able to convince him to do a favor for me and host the event.

"That would be terrific, Jax. You'll ask him?"

"I will, but I can't promise he'll say yes," I replied. "Oh, and Tessa? You should know that Zachary says Austin was murdered. It was no accident."

"*Che casino!*" Tessa said, switching into her native Italian, which she often did in times of stress or when she was drunk. "I figured as much. But, I'm not going to tell the girls that. They're already bonkers without knowing that—"

"Um, Tessa? Do you realize we left five unsupervised teen girls in the basement?" We jumped to our feet and bolted back down the stairs to the rehearsal room, but the girls were nowhere in sight. There was a door at the far end of the room, and it was ajar. We opened the door and peered down a long, dark hallway crowded with boxes and props. Stepping cautiously into the hall, we listened for any signs that the girls had headed this way.

Suddenly there was a squeak, followed by the girls' screams, and then the sound of teens sprinting toward us. Realizing they might not see us in the dark, and fearing we were about to be trampled by a herd of panicked girls, I turned and bolted back toward the brightly-lit rehearsal room. After reaching the room, I realized Tessa wasn't with me. She had continued into the tunnel to find the girls. Seconds later, they came running toward me, still squealing with fright, as Tessa herded them from behind. They piled through the door and slammed it shut. Tessa was breathing heavily as she leaned against the door.

"Ew! Mom! It was a rat," Izzy said, in a voice almost as high-pitched as the rat's squeal we'd heard moments before.

Tessa stood there, silently staring at the girls squeezed together in a tight cluster.

"Sorry, Mom. We've never been in the Underground before," Ashley said, realizing they had more to be worried about than a rodent, like their mother's wrath.

"The Underground? We're in the Underground?" I asked. I'd heard there was a series of passageways beneath the city of Seattle. There were even tours that would take people into these places. I'd never been on one of the tours because, frankly, I wasn't keen on small, dark places. What I knew about the Underground was that after the great Seattle fire of 1889, which destroyed 31 city blocks, the merchants started rebuilding immediately. Seattle was originally built too close to sea level, so in the years immediately following the fire, Seattle re-graded the entire city, raising up the downtown area by several feet, and bringing the surrounding hills down several feet. After the re-grading was complete, the merchants simply closed their shops on the lower levels and opened their new front doors on the upper levels. Those lower levels are now known as the Seattle Underground.

"Maybe I'll take you on a tour someday. That would be much safer," Tessa said, blowing her bangs from her forehead, a sure sign of her impatience. "Now, we only have a few more days to get ready for the gala. I thought maybe we would work on the bidding cards and organizing the auction items."

"What are we going to do about the jewelry? Frankie took it all," I reminded Tessa.

"We're going to have to find some new jewelry then. It shouldn't be too hard—we make jewelry for a living. Frankie hasn't cornered the market on handmade necklaces," Tessa said.

"You can put me in charge of the jewelry. I'll get enough pieces for everyone," I replied.

"And Mom? Mr. Greer said he was going to do our makeup. Not that we, like, wanted him to, but now, who's going to do it?" Izzy asked.

"Jax?" Tessa asked.

"Not me. All I use is tinted lip balm and bronzer," I said. Izzy gave me a pitying look, thinking, I was certain, that I was seriously flawed if that was all I knew about makeup.

"Do you think Val could help?" Tessa asked me.

"I'll ask her. I bet she'll say yes. Any opportunity to do something glamorous and she's all in."

"Thanks," Tessa said, giving me a big hug.

"I'm going to get out of here. Zachary will probably show up soon to continue his investigation today. I don't want to see him in his stern detective mood. Besides, I have jewelry to find for all these outfits." I had Tessa hold up each outfit on its hanger while I took pictures with my phone. The images would be helpful references as I went on my quest to find jewelry for the models to wear with the clothing. I left Tessa to wrangle the girls—she was much better at it than I was. I made my way out of the theater. As I crossed Yesler Square, I saw a familiar government-issued black sedan pulling to the curb. I ducked behind the statue of Henry Yesler, but it was too late. Zachary had seen me.

SIX

"THERE'S NO USE in trying to hide," Zachary shouted to me from the open window of his car. "I spotted you from a block away."

"Fine." I came out from my hiding place. "I was hoping you weren't going to see me at the scene of the crime. I want you to know I am not getting involved in any way. I've got a job to do. I'm working with Tessa on a fashion show. I'm finding necklaces to go with some of the outfits the models are wearing. That's all."

"Glad you're going to leave it to the professionals this time around." I had an urge to stick my tongue out at him, but I knew he would think I was being immature. Besides, at that very moment, he cracked a huge smile, the one that makes the corners of his eyes crinkle, and I got all mushy inside. Zachary and I had had some challenges in the last year that we'd known each other. I'd gotten involved in a couple of murder investigations, and he hadn't been pleased with me about that. He really didn't want me trying to do his job. In the end, I'd helped him solve a few crimes, but he still didn't like it when I meddled. "So, I take it that means the show must go on?"

"Until we hear otherwise, we're carrying on with the gala," I said, pausing for a moment to focus on him. "Do you want to stop over later? I could pick up some Chinese food."

"I'd love to, but this may take a while. I'll call you," Zachary said, rolling up his window and cruising down the street to find a parking spot. I was glad I was only going to work on the auction and fashion show, and didn't have to worry about Zachary getting angry when I did my own snooping. I was certain that would put stress on our newly-formed relationship. He was, and would always be, the stern detective I met last year. And while I hoped to soften him up, at least when he was alone with me, I knew I could never change his demeanor when he was on the job.

● ● ●

Back at home, I got organized for my treasure hunt. I needed to find jewelry for ten outfits—two for each of the five girls. I pulled out my phone and looked at the pictures of the clothing. The first outfit was an emerald green tunic with stripes of yellow and red running randomly through the sheer raw silk fabric. It had been paired with skinny black jeans. I rummaged around in my stock of jewelry and found a lovely necklace to go with the outfit: a teardrop-shaped pendant in black with swirls of green and yellow. It coordinated perfectly. I pulled out another necklace, this one featuring lampworked beads in red with black polka dots and black with red polka dots. As I looked at the piece, I realized it was one of my favorites. I decided to keep this one, and took to it my bedroom and put it away. As I continued to look through my inventory, I found a necklace that would be great for one of the teen models—it was a long strand of emerald green beads with silver foil encased with clear glass. I wasn't sure which outfit this piece would go with, but I was certain it would be spectacular. Two necklaces down and eight to go. This was going to take some time. Fortunately, I had a few days to get it figured out.

Gumdrop leaped onto the worktable and flopped over onto the jewelry I had brought out.

"Sorry, Gummie, this is not the best place for you. You'll knock these necklaces on the floor, and that would be a disaster." I picked up my cat and carried him to the kitchen, setting him down on the counter while I got him some food. I knew I shouldn't put him on the kitchen counter, but I lived alone. I washed my counters often, so it wasn't too bad, especially with no witnesses other than Gumdrop—and he wasn't going to tell anyone. "Are you hungry?" I asked my cat.

"Yello?" Gumdrop said, pacing along the edge of the counter.

"Are you asking for catnip?"

"Yello. Yello?" he meowed again.

"Okay, you've been pretty good. I guess you can have some." My cat was a little drug addict. I was the one who got him hooked. He loved the tiny catnip-infused ice cubes I made for him. I pulled a cube out of the pink plastic tray I kept in the freezer and placed it in a bowl on the counter next to him. "Here you go, big boy."

Gumdrop looked down at the cube and sniffed it. Something was wrong. He wasn't going crazy. Any other time, he tended to go bonkers when I gave him one of his favorite catnip ice cubes. I picked him up, carried him to the sofa, and examined him. He didn't look well. I hadn't noticed before, but his eyes looked watery and he was sniffling a little. Gumdrop was sick.

I called my new vet's office. Fortunately, his schedule was light for that day. The receptionist told me to bring Gumdrop in right away.

I picked Gummie up, put him in his carrier, and headed out the back door. He got to ride shotgun in the front seat, and soon we were speeding toward the veterinary office of Dr. Buff Brown. He'd replaced my old vet, Dr. Diaz, after he retired.

Dr. Brown's office was like most veterinary practices, with basic white floors and counters. What made it stand out was its artwork. Instead of the usual puppies and kitties in framed posters on the walls, there were beautiful, artistic photographs of our feline and canine friends, which added an air of sophistication to the clinic.

"Hi, I'm Jax O'Connell and this is Gumdrop," I told the receptionist as I approached the front desk and set Gummie's carrier on the floor. "Thanks so much for giving us an appointment on such short notice."

"Dr. Brown will be right with you," said the receptionist, a young woman with neon pink hair sticking out in all directions. It looked like she'd woken up, looked in the mirror and been so surprised to discover her hair had turned pink that it stood straight up in shock. The woman picked up Gumdrop's carrier, handed me a clipboard full of forms, and asked me to fill them out while she escorted me to the exam room.

I pulled Gumdrop out of his carrier and put him on the metal exam table then sat down to fill out the paperwork. Immediately, he jumped into my lap and pressed himself up against me. I gave him long strokes down his back while admiring a lovely framed photo of a dramatically lit dachshund on the wall.

"Oh, Gummie, please be okay," I said, kissing the top of his furry little head. I dutifully filled out the forms the receptionist had given me while I waited for the vet.

"Dr. Buff Brown, nice to meet you," the vet said, entering the exam room. Buff was not a traditional kind of handsome. But there was something about this man—call it animal magnetism, although that was an all-too-obvious thing to say about a vet. He was tall and solid, his gray-blue eyes almost too cool to look at directly, a bald head, and full, dark beard. Somehow, that bald head suited him. The beard? It was impressive, if you were into that sort of thing. There was something playful about him, like he'd be ready at the drop of a hat to go out and play fetch, and it wouldn't only be to please the dog.

I placed my cat back on the exam table, and the vet put out his hand for Gumdrop to sniff. My cat sauntered over and pressed his furry little head into Dr. Brown's open hand.

"Now, then, who's a nice cat?" the vet asked Gumdrop, giving him a little scratch on the chin. Dr. Brown's obvious love of animals was very appealing. Of course, I was dating Zachary, so the vet wasn't in the running for me, but I wondered if Val might be interested in him. She usually favored a traditional-type of handsome and would not necessarily like the looks of Buff Brown. But, if she could look beyond his not-quite-GQ exterior, I thought she might be impressed, or at least intrigued.

"And how is Gumdrop doing?" the vet asked. I noticed his Southern drawl and wondered if Val would like his accent. Oh dear, had I become a matchmaker?

"He doesn't look like he's feeling well. I'm worried about him."

"It does look like he's got some eye discharge here," the doctor said, looking at Gummie's face, while deftly taking the cat's temperature by sticking a digital thermometer in his ear. "And it looks like he has a little bit of a fever. Has he been eating?"

"Not really, but he's always been a picky eater. I knew something was wrong when he didn't go crazy with the catnip treat I like to give him. Usually, he goes nuts, but today he just looked at it and said *yello*."

"'Yello?' Is that normal for him?"

"Yes, it is." Gumdrop flopped down on the table and sneezed. Poor boy.

"And has he been around any other animals that might not be up to date on their vaccines?"

"No. He's an inside cat, and he doesn't really like other animals."

"Hm. I thought perhaps he might have a virus, but he would need to be around other animals to have caught something."

"He's sometimes around my neighbor Val's dog, but he's had all his shots."

"We need to do some tests so we can figure out what's going on with your kitty and get him on the road to recovery." The vet pinched Gummie's fur. "It looks like he might be a bit dehydrated. We need to get a blood sample, run some tests, and give him some subcutaneous fluids. It could take a while. Why don't you leave him here with us. I promise we'll take good care of him."

"Okay. Just give me a call when it's time for me to pick him up." I gathered up the clipboard and my handbag. "You be nice to the doctor," I said to my cat. Gummie, still on the exam table, sauntered over to the vet and started purring. My cat didn't usually like men, so this was a positive sign. When Gummie doesn't like someone, he's been known to cause quite a ruckus.

"Well! Aren't you full of surprises!" Dr. Brown said as he scratched my cat between his ears. "We'll give you a call toward the end of the day to give you an update. Thanks for bringing him in." The vet hoisted Gumdrop off the exam table to take him into the back room.

I dropped the clipboard with the completed forms on the receptionist's desk. The woman with shocking pink hair was on the phone and nodded thanks as I left. Back outside in the daylight, I decided to take a walk and pull myself together. I was upset Gummie was sick and hoped it was nothing serious.

As I walked down Jackson Street toward Second Ave South, I passed Chu's Antiquities. The owner, Mr. Chu, was my next-door neighbor. I'd always been curious about his shop but had never made the time to come down and explore it. Deciding that today was as good a day as any, I went inside. I did have an ulterior motive. Perhaps he'd want to help our cause by donating a necklace for the fashion show. Mr. Chu liked cats more than people, and had dozens of them—cats, not people—in his house across the alley from mine. Tessa and I had entered his house last month, and we'd been relieved to discover that while he did have an unreasonable number of cats, his home didn't smell like a litter box, and all his animals seemed to be happy and healthy.

The bell on the door to Mr. Chu's shop jingled faintly as I entered. His store was dimly lit, and it was hard to move through the crowded and meandering aisles. The distinctive musty smell of antiques was as thick as the dust on the highest shelves. As I walked through the aisles, I was astounded by the amazing collection of items he had in his shop: vintage rattan bird cages, stacks of antique books, china figurines, exotic musical instruments, and so much more. I could have spent the rest of the day browsing the unusual items in his shop. But not today. Today I was on a mission to find at least one more necklace to go with an outfit for the fashion show. I was feeling pretty down in the dumps—more in the mood for a stiff drink than a shopping excursion. I knew Gummie was going to be okay, but I was still worried about him, and worried about the cost of vet bill as well.

I finally located Mr. Chu at a small, crowded desk in the back of the shop, a cloud of pine-scented smoke surrounding him. Usually he wasn't wearing much more than a robe and boxer shorts, but today—appropriately, since he was in his place of business—he was wearing slate gray dress pants that were a little too baggy and a plain white button-down shirt with a white undershirt peeking out at the neckline. It was the first time I had seen him without a cat in his lap.

He must not have heard me enter, since he didn't greet me.

"Excuse me, Mr. Chu?" I said.

"You here to buy something?" he said, glancing up at me, then returning his focus to his work. "Because if not, you should stick to bothering me at home, okay?"

"I was here to ask you a favor—"

"This is a place of business, not favors," he said, turning his attention back to his work. A small puff of smoke swirled away from the soldering iron tip he was holding to a bead on a strand.

"What are you doing?" I asked, peering over his shoulder.

"Nothing important. You're bothering me. I'm busy."

"What if the favor you did for me meant you could advertise your shop to a large group of wealthy people attending a charity auction and fashion show?" I asked.

He said nothing, so I took a deep breath and kept going.

"We're having an auction and the proceeds go to a nonprofit organization that helps the homeless. There's a fashion show, and I'm in charge of putting together jewelry with the clothing. I know it's for people and not cats, but I was hoping—"

"I like people just fine, but cats seem to like me better than people do. But, if you think it will mean I get some new customers, I'll consider it." Mr. Chu pressed the tip of the hot soldering iron into the hole of another dark yellow bead. The smell of burnt oil wafted by me.

"Aha! This one is fake," he said, pulling the bead off the strand and setting it in a white ceramic bowl. "These so-called amber beads, I test them to see if they're real. I give them a little heat right in the hole, and if I smell pine then the bead is real amber."

"Why do they smell like pine?"

"Don't you know anything about beads?"

"I know a lot about glass beads, not as much about other kinds," I admitted. I recalled that Mr. Chu, who usually was an expert at identifying antiques, had sent me on a wild goose chase when he misidentified some beads Tessa and I had shown him last month.

"Amber is fossilized tree sap. If I heat it up, it will smell like a forest in here." He pressed the soldering iron tip to another bead, and the smoke emitted the sweet scent of a pine tree.

"Another real one," I said, sniffing the aroma of pine sap.

"Yes, and that's the last one. Out of this strand, only one is fake. That's acceptable. Now, what would you want for this auction of yours?"

"Do you have an amber necklace we could use?" I had in mind a flowing lavender gown with pale yellow flowers that would look terrific with a necklace made of amber beads.

"I have just the thing." Mr. Chu shuffled over to a door and opened it. "You come with me." He reached inside the door and flipped a switch to illuminate a dark, narrow staircase heading down. This was not my idea of a good time. I hoped Tessa would appreciate the lengths I was willing to go to for the sake of the event.

"What is this place?" I asked, but I knew the answer even before I'd even finished asking the question.

"This is my storage room. Used to be part of the Underground."

I hesitated. Mr. Chu turned around and looked up at me.

"Come on, come on. There's no boogeyman down here," he said, beckoning me with one of his weathered hands. Cautiously, I followed him, keeping my head low so I didn't end up with a face full of cobwebs.

When we reached the bottom of the stairs, Mr. Chu fumbled for the light switch. The light came on, illuminating a small, dingy space not much larger than my bedroom. The room was lined with shelves, which were filled with neatly labeled boxes. He might have had a lot of stuff, but at least he was organized.

"Here's what I was looking for," Mr. Chu said, pulling a small box from a shelf. He opened the box and pulled out a choker-length necklace of chunky amber orbs with tiny gold beads mixed in between them and an antique clasp in the shape of a lotus flower. "Will this work? They're not real amber. Otherwise, they'd be worth a fortune. But it's a nice piece. It should sell for a good price."

"It's perfect! Thank you!" I said, reaching over to hug him.

"All right already," he said, waving me away. I backed off, remembering he simply wasn't the hugging type.

"The model will wear it in the fashion show, and we'll tell the audience who donated it. We're offering the donors half the proceeds of the auction price, plus a ticket to the auction. Okay?" I doubted I could get him to come to the gala, but it was worth a try.

"Let me get this wrapped up for you," he said, as I followed him back up the stairs, and not a minute too soon. I was starting to sweat down there, and not because I was hot. I couldn't stand being in that dark place, wondering what kind of creepy-crawlies might be headed up my pant leg. "I'm not so sure about coming to the event, I've got a lot to tend to at home." I was sure what he meant was he had a lot of cats to tend to. But I hoped he'd come, if for no other reason than to get someone else to fill a seat in the large venue. Perhaps he'd even bid on some auction items.

Mr. Chu might have been a grumpy old man, but I knew deep down inside he was a sweetheart.

SEVEN

WITH THE PACKAGE from Mr. Chu containing the faux-amber necklace tucked safely into my handbag, I walked back to the vet's office but hesitated by the door. Since they wouldn't have any test results yet, I knew it was useless to check in.

I got in my car and flipped down the sun visor, then opened its mirror to check for any spider webs that might have stuck to my hair while I was down in the Underground. While I liked to believe there was no real reason why I was afraid of dark, spooky places, the truth was I'd experienced a traumatic event as a kid, and I still hadn't completely recovered. Memories of the childhood incident that caused my fear of spiders came rushing back.

• • •

My brother Andy, sister Connie, and I had a pretty normal childhood growing up in Miami. Long before Andy was born, our mother would throw Connie and me outside to play, especially when the weather was balmy. One of our favorite games was hide and seek. I remember once hiding in what I considered the very best spot of all—in our family's hurricane shelter. Living in Florida, we had to be prepared for tropical storms, and my dad had built a small hurricane shelter beneath our house for that eventuality. The door to the shelter was outside of the house, below the kitchen window. Usually the door was locked, but for some reason, it was unlocked that day. I seem to recall my dad had been restocking some of the supplies around that time and may have simply forgotten to lock up when he was finished.

Opening the door just far enough to accommodate my six-year-old self, I slipped inside. I'd never been in the shelter before, at least that I remembered. My mother had talked about using it for a Category Five storm when I was a baby, but I didn't remember that, of course.

As I hid in the dark, I waited for my sister to find my superb hiding spot. I waited, and waited, and waited. And she never came. It was dark in the shelter and while I was pretty sure there was a light somewhere down there, I didn't want to explore too much. My imagination started to take over. There were some webs here and there, but my young brain kicked into overdrive and I convinced myself that the cramped space was home to thousands of spiders that were crawling up my legs and arms. I was so freaked out I gave up on hiding and pushed on the door to open it. But it wouldn't budge. I tried and tried to open the door. In a panic, with my heart racing, I flung myself against the door over and over, bruising my shoulder. Finally giving up, I sat on the top step crying, certain no one would ever find me alive. I convinced myself I'd be wound up in webs and eaten by spiders.

When my mother wrenched open the shelter door a few minutes before dinner, I was certain she would be relieved to find me, uneaten by the monster spiders, which of course, had grown in my imagination the longer I sat in the shelter. Instead of sweeping me into her arms, relieved to find me, she yanked me out of the shelter, scolded me for having gone in there in the first place, and sent me off to take a bath, which I was relieved to do. I wanted nothing more than to get the spider webs off my head.

• • •

My next stop was Rosie Paredes' bead shop. Aztec Beads was located in the middle of Wallingford, one of the hipper neighborhoods in Seattle. The building was painted vibrant red, with a sign at the corner that had the image of an Aztec figure lying on his back holding a full tray of beads aloft, as if making an offering to the gods. It was Tessa's and my favorite bead shop, though Rosie wasn't always the most pleasant person to deal with.

"Hi, Rosie," I said, entering the shop to find her stocking tiny vials of seed beads into a display by the cash register.

"Look, I know why you're here and the answer is no," Rosie said, pushing her pudgy hand at me in the universal palm-out sign for STOP as I came in the door.

"How could you possibly know?"

"Frankie Lawton, that's how. He called me and said someone would be coming by and groveling for some jewelry for that fashion show, and it would be in my best interest to say no."

"Why would he do that? I don't get it. I don't even understand why he left."

"Jax, you don't want to get involved with those Greers. I know they do a lot of good in the community, but there's more there than meets the eye. You can't trust them. Trust me."

"Mr. Greer was a little odd, maybe. But I don't—"

"Look, you've just got to trust me on this one. I trust Frankie, I've known him for years. If he says it's too dangerous, it's way too dangerous." Frankie was, in my opinion, a giant pain in the butt, so it was difficult for me to consider much of anything he said as valid.

As if to punctuate Rosie's warning, her little Chihuahua-wolverine mutt, Tito, ran up to me and started barking and snapping at my sneakers. The little black and white dog's bulging eyes glared at me with a fierce intensity that told me his bite just might be worse than his bark. I flicked my foot at him, and the dog backed off, growling as he did. I swear I didn't kick him.

"Okay, thanks for the heads-up," I said, dancing out the door to avoid Tito as he advanced again, nipping at my heels. Back inside the Ladybug, I called Tessa.

"I just had the oddest conversation with Rosie. Why would Frankie think the Greers were dangerous?"

"No idea."

"So, what do you think? Is it too dangerous for you to be there, especially with your girls?"

"There haven't been any more falling chandeliers, so that's good news."

"What an awful thought," I said, thinking about how horrible it would be to die that way.

"How's it going with the necklace treasure hunt?" Tessa asked.

"I've made a little progress. I've got two necklaces I made and one from Mr. Chu. But Rosie turned me down cold. Apparently, Frankie Lawton warned her to stay away from the whole mess."

"That's strange, don't you think?" Tessa asked.

"A little, but then, Frankie is a little strange."

Tessa laughed, which was good to hear for a change. This event was taking its toll on her, especially now that we didn't have Austin or Frankie to ride roughshod over everyone.

"Uh-oh. I think we've got trouble." Tessa's voice was suddenly taut with anxiety.

"Trouble? What kind of trouble?" I asked, as I started the Ladybug and got ready to roll.

"You need to get over here. Right now." Tessa hung up the phone.

I sped to the theater. As I entered the backstage, I saw Zachary sitting in the wings with Tessa's daughters and the other models. All the girls were crying and Zachary looked uncomfortable as he scribbled in his notebook, trying not to make eye contact with them. Tessa was staring fiercely at Zachary as she stood behind the girls. I was sure he had made her daughters and their friends cry. I wanted to stay out of Zachary's way, and I thought it best to let him interview the girls without being distracted by me. Tessa spotted me and gave me a tiny wave, but I just kept moving. I cut across the stage and found Daniel Owens backstage fussing with the lamp I'd given him.

"Hi, Daniel, how are you doing?"

Daniel looked up at me from where he was crouching as he attached wheels to my former light fixture.

"As good as can be expected. Thanks for the lamp. It's going to work perfectly as our new ghost light. Although we might not need it for long. We may have to close our doors for good now that we don't have Austin," Daniel said, as he screwed a new light bulb into the fixture.

"It seems like Tessa's got things under control with the fashion show and auction. Is everything going okay with *Hamlet*? That's on track, isn't it?"

"Yes, but Austin usually looked at the books right around this time of the month and made a donation if we were having a cash flow problem. We don't always stay afloat with just our ticket sales. With him gone, I'm not sure what we'll do." Daniel stood up and swiveled the lamp around on its new wheels, admiring his work.

"I wish there was something else I could do for you. Did HAT owe the theater money for the rental that might help you make ends meet? I could talk with Jaya—"

"No, Austin gave them the rental for free. He did that a lot. I don't think he had a good head for money."

"I'm so sorry." I spotted Zachary crossing the stage, having finished his interrogation of the teens. "Excuse me, I need to talk to that detective." I trotted toward Zachary.

"What are you doing here?" he asked.

"I was about to ask you the same thing," I said.

"I'm investigating a homicide, which is my job. You, on the other hand, said you were going to stay far away from this investigation."

"I am, but I'm still a volunteer for the gala. And, you'll notice I didn't get anywhere near you when you were interviewing the girls."

"I appreciate that, but your presence here doesn't make it any easier for me to do my job." Zachary's mood seemed especially dark, It was time to distract him the only way I knew how, at least in public.

"Come on, let's go get a cup of coffee. My treat." I grabbed Zachary's hand and we headed out the door to the Starbucks across Yesler Square from the theater. Once we were out in the sunshine Zachary's mood improved, and he seemed to loosen up a bit. I bought us each a coffee and we found a seat on a bench in the shade of one of the maples in the square.

"So…" I started slowly. "How did it go with the girls?"

Zachary sighed and looked into his cup.

"The girls were impossible. I questioned them, and they were almost entirely unwilling to speak. All they did is cry. They didn't answer a single question, except for Izzy. She seems to have become their spokesgirl."

"And what did she have to say?" I asked.

"She didn't have one nice thing to say about Austin Greer."

"Not too surprising."

"Why do you say that?" Zachary said, looking me in the eye, truly curious about what secret knowledge I held that he was clueless about.

"Two things: First, how much time have you spent around teen girls?"

"Not much. You know I was an only child. And I didn't really date in high school, or really ever."

"Okay, well, teen girls can be overly emotional, sullen, flighty, and verbose—all in the span of five minutes. I'm sure they were scared, talking with you, and they just shut down."

"You said two things. What's the other?"

"Did you ever meet Austin Greer? Because if you did, you'd know he was an odd bird, and in the short amount of time I was with him, he was rude, bossy, and at times unpleasant. I know those are not good reasons to kill someone, but it is why you're not hearing anything positive from the teens."

"Well, the girls not talking to me is not great for them. It certainly means we have to consider them as suspects until they can explain themselves."

"You can't be serious. They're just kids."

"That's the problem. None of the kids liked this man, and when someone turns up dead, we have to look around at the most obvious suspects. And it's not only Izzy and Ashley, it's all the girls who are part of this event. I'm afraid they're all considered suspects."

"Five high school girls?"

"I'm afraid so."

"Would it help if I talked with them? You could even be with me when it happened. All those girls know me. Maybe they'd be willing to open up. That would help, right?"

"Jax, I don't know how to say this, but I don't need your help." He reached out to take my hand. "Please understand."

"You know what? That's just fine." I stood up. I was done with this conversation. "I don't need to be involved in this case. You've got it handled. You don't need me. Right?"

"Right."

And that was it. I swallowed hard and walked away. Angry and sad at the same time, I got in my car and drove home. My head and my heart ached. He didn't need me. And what did I need? Right then, I needed some chocolate.

EIGHT

ENTERING THE BACK DOOR of my house, I instinctively looked around the studio for Gumdrop. Remembering he was still at the vet's office, I gave Dr. Brown a call.

"Ah, yes, Gumdrop. He's doing well. We haven't gotten any of our lab results back yet, but we've given him some fluids, and he is perking up nicely," Buff Brown said with a slow drawl.

"Can I come get him and bring him home?"

"I think so. No harm in him being home. Oh, I noticed from your paperwork that you live in the Queen Anne District. I'm on my way home and could easily drop him off. Would that be okay with you?"

"Oh, I, of course," I said, stunned the vet would be willing to bring Gummie back to me.

After hanging up with the vet, I made a cup of coffee and sat on my sofa and thought about my conversation with Zachary. I was upset with him, of course, but I was upset with myself, as well. I'd offered my help to him, after telling him I was going to stay away from the investigation, and he'd refused it. Even though I'd had some success in the past solving murder cases, I needed to remember it wasn't my job. I wasn't sure why I needed to seek justice when someone died at the hands of a killer, but it was important to me. It was a way I could bring order to the world, in a small way. And this was a big, messy world, one I'd never make sense of. All this deep thinking was making me blue, so I did the one thing that always cheered me up. I went to see Val. It occurred to me that I could invite her to my house so I could introduce her to Dr. Brown, if she was willing. And Val was always willing to meet a new man.

"Jax, shweetie!" Val slurred, swinging the door open wide. "Come on in!"

"Are you day drinking?" I asked, since Val seemed to be acting crazier than usual.

"No—I mean—yes. But not enough to be drunk, at least not yet. I want you to meet my friend Rudy."

"Yes, I've met Rudy several times. He painted my kitchen, remember? He worked on Tessa's house. He's your sci-fi buddy." Rudy waved from his perch on Val's bright pink sofa. A Star Wars film was playing on the television, the volume turned up a little too loud.

"We've been playing a drinking game. So far, Rudy's winning," Val said, stumbling over and whacking him on the knee with her open palm, nearly falling off her shiny blue stilettos. Val was in no condition to meet anyone. She was absolutely snockered.

"You going to join us, Jax? We're still on the first movie. That's episode four, but it was the first movie. It's one of the best. Because, you know, episode one, it was horrible—it had the stupid Jar Jar Binks character. There's still time for you to play," Val said, as Rudy poured another drink into the shot glass in her outstretched hand.

"What are you playing?"

"May the Fourth," Val slurred.

"No, it's May the Force," Rudy said.

"No, today's date, it's May the Fourth. It's the game you play today. It's the Star Wars drinking game. We're not entirely sure how to win—maybe whoever doesn't pass out wins," Val said.

"I thought you were on the Werewolf Diet. Weren't you supposed to only drink clear liquids today?"

"Yes. And here's the thing: Vodka is a clear liquid. So strictly speaking, I am working within the guidelines of the diet. Besides, what do werewolves really know about losing weight?"

I had no idea how to respond to any number of the assertions Val had made. Rudy looked over at us, puzzled, then downed another shot of liquor.

"How do you even play this silly game?" I asked.

"See, what you do is, when someone says something like, 'I have a bad feeling about this,' we take a drink," Val said, filling her glass with vodka and tossing it back to demonstrate. "Woo!" She shook her head and stumbled before steading herself on the back of the sofa.

"You know, I'd love to stay, but I can see you are both pretty busy, and I don't want to intrude," I said, heading for the door. Stanley, Val's basset hound, bounded after me. The poor dog seemed a bit frantic, with all the noise from the movie and Val and Rudy being pretty loud themselves. "I'm taking Stanley with me."

"Okay, sweet cheeks," Val said, plopping herself down on the sofa next to Rudy while he filled their glasses again. I'd have to do my matchmaking between Val and Dr. Brown some other day.

Grabbing Stanley by the collar, I opened Val's front door. As I made a U-turn back into my house, I spotted Dr. Brown cruising down the street on a Harley with an unusual sidecar attached to it. He parked it at the curb in front of my duplex.

I stood there, my mouth gaping.

"Wow. Nice motorcycle—is that custom?"

"I've been working on it for a while. This way I can make house calls in style," Dr. Brown said, grinning with pride. He unlocked the carrier from the sidecar and pulled it out. "And Gumdrop here didn't seem to mind a bit."

I peered into the carrier. Gumdrop, who was a notoriously bad traveler, seemed to be having a fine time despite looking a little windblown around the edges. Usually he'd howl anytime I had to take him in the car. Instead, it sounded like he was purring. I'd have to remember that the next time I took him for a ride—perhaps I could leave the top down in the Ladybug to give him a feeling of wide open spaces and wind rushing through his fur.

"Let's get my biker-cat inside," I said with a giggle.

Dr. Brown, carrying Gumdrop in his carrier, followed me inside, while I parked Stanley next to the kitchen table.

"Nice-looking basset hound you got there," he said, admiring Stanley.

"Oh, thanks. He lives next door. Actually, I have joint custody of him, but he spends most of his time with my neighbor Val because Gummie doesn't like Stanley much." I gave the dog a couple of pats on his side, and his fat tail thumped the wood floor in response.

Dr. Brown put the carrier on the table and opened it. Gummie slunk out. He looked down at Stanley and hissed. Instead of making a beeline for one of his favorite spots—the paisley chair—he stayed on the table, out of the dog's reach.

"Nice house you have here. I bought a house a lot like this one a few blocks away last month. A real fixer-upper. Looks like you've been working on yours," Dr. Brown said, admiring the living room and kitchen.

"I updated the rental unit next door first; now I'm playing catch-up with my side. I'm getting ready to renovate the attic. We're starting work on it this week," I said, giving Gummie some long pets down his back. "Any updates on Gumdrop?"

"We'll have the lab results tomorrow, but other than being a little dehydrated, he seems like he is doing okay. Speaking of dehydrated, might I—"

"Oh, can I get you something to drink? Please make yourself comfortable," I said, gesturing to my vintage velvet sofa.

"If it's not too much trouble." Buff settled onto the sofa.

"Water? A beer? Wine? Those are pretty much the only choices unless you want coffee."

"I wouldn't want to impose. Water is fine."

"After the day I've had, a glass of wine sounds marvelous. Are you sure I can't get you a glass?"

"Okay, if you're going to twist my arm," Buff said with a bark of a laugh. "As long it's red."

"It is." I found two glasses and reopened the bottle of pinot noir left over from a couple of nights ago. I poured us each a glass of wine.

Gumdrop let out a loud *yello*.

"Oh, are you hungry now? Did Dr. Brown—"

"Call me Buff," the vet said.

"Okay, then, did Buff feed you?" I asked the cat. I took a moment to put some of Gummie's favorite savory salmon canned cat food into his bowl and set it on the table next to him. He sniffed it and walked away. "Dammit, Gummie, please eat." I picked him up and turned him around, so he was facing his food bowl.

"As long as he's drinking, I think it's okay if he doesn't eat much. He's got plenty of meat on his bones to keep him going for quite some time."

"Are you telling me my cat is fat?" I joked.

"He's just right. I'm certain he'll bounce back quickly. So, don't worry," he said with a smile.

As I crossed the kitchen with the wine, my foot skidded in something wet—Stanley's drool, most likely. Red wine from one of the glasses splashed across the front of my blouse.

"Oh, no!" I set the glasses down on the kitchen table. "I'll be right back. Please help yourself to the wine." I slipped into the bathroom and pulled off my blouse then rinsed it in the sink to get the red wine out of it. I'd have to do a better job before the stain set, but for now, it was going to have to do. I wrapped a towel around my chest and got ready to bolt for my bedroom.

The doorbell rang. I shouted to Buff, asking him to answer the door. I hoped it was Val, because I wanted her to meet Dr. Brown. Although, since she was more than a little tipsy, I was uncertain what she might do, especially if she was interested in him. With only my bra on and a towel clutched to my chest, I poked my head out the bathroom door. No such luck. It wasn't Val. It was Zachary. Oh dear.

I resisted the urge to squeal and instead sped into my bedroom and shut the door. I grabbed a T-shirt from the dresser drawer, slipped it on, and then skidded into the hallway.

"Zachary. So nice of you to stop by. Listen, I, uh. You're not going to believe this, but..."

I was stumped. Did I tell him that Buff Brown was in my living room with a glass of wine after making a house call with Gumdrop? Or should I send Zachary away with no explanation at all?

After opening the door, Buff had settled down on the couch with his wine glass. Stanley was sitting at his feet. Zachary's face showed no emotion, but I knew he must be upset. "I see you have company. I best be on my way," Zachary said, turning to go.

"No, Zachary, don't go. Let me explain," I touched his arm, trying to make a connection and stop him from leaving.

"Oh, I think it's pretty obvious. No need to explain." And then he was gone.

I closed the door and turned back to Buff.

"Boyfriend trouble?" he asked, nodding toward the now-closed door.

"We hit a bit of a rough spot earlier today. I don't think what just happened improved things much."

"I'm sure you can explain it all to him, and he'll come around," he said. "So, Jax, what do you do for a living?"

"I'm a glass beadmaker."

"You're kidding. Oddly enough, I've been looking for someone who makes glass beads."

"I've got my studio here at my house. Want to see it?"

"Sure," he said, following me down the hall to my studio.

"Why have you wanted to find a glass beadmaker? Not that many people know about it."

"When I was at the old animal clinic in South Seattle, I used to buy beautiful dog jewelry from a woman named Marta, but somehow, she seems to have fallen off the face of the earth. A lot of my clients have been asking about her dog necklaces, and I'd love to carry some in my new practice."

Marta was a glass beadmaker who had stayed at my house during the grand opening weekend of Aztec Beads last year. While Marta seemed nice, she certainly had some dark secrets that shocked us all when they were revealed. In fact, Stanley had belonged to Marta. I was surprised Buff hadn't recognized the dog, but I supposed he met a lot of animals, and he obviously couldn't remember all of them.

I showed Buff my torch and all of my tools, as well as my beads stacked in boxes in every available nook and cranny.

"Can you make me a bead?" Buff asked.

"Sure. How about I make one with a little paw print on it?"

"That would be spectacular." He settled into a chair next to my workbench.

I started by turning on the natural gas and the oxygen to my torch, then lighting it. A perfect eight-inch-long blue flame burst from the tip of the torch.

"Okay, so now that I have my torch set just right, I'll melt some red glass in the flame, and I'll make a base bead." Once I had a big enough blob of molten glass, I wrapped it around a mandrel—a stiff metal wire covered with a clay-like substance. I shaped the glass in the flame until it formed a flat disk.

"Now I'll add an ivory paw print." I added a pea-sized polka dot of glass and used a tungsten pick to give it the distinctive heart-shaped center of a paw and added four smaller dots of glass to make the toes. Then I melted them all in.

"That looks terrific, Jax," Buff said. "Maybe you can make more for me. I'll figure out what I want and then place an order, okay?"

"That would be fantastic," I said, placing the bead into my kiln.

•   •   •

After Buff left, I found Gumdrop still sitting on the kitchen table, looking down disdainfully at Stanley who was snoozing on the floor below him. I grabbed my cat and brought him over to the sofa.

"How are you doing, big fella?" I asked as he arranged himself in my lap. He replied with a purr and by sinking his nails into my thigh. I stifled a yelp and took a swig of my pinot, then I screwed up my courage and called Zachary. The call went straight to voicemail.

"Hey, hi, it's Jax. I wanted to say that there is really no need for you to be upset. That guy was my vet, I mean, Gumdrop's vet. Okay, bye," I said, adding, "please call me back."

Tessa called a few minutes later.

"How are things going with the gala?" I asked.

"Terrible! With Austin Greer's death, his wife has decided to pull the plug on the event and close the theater."

"They can't do that! And what about *Hamlet*? They're going to shut that down as well?"

"Amanda Greer said that without Austin, she doesn't want to keep the theater open. I'm not sure what happens with *Hamlet*, but it is a tragedy." I wasn't sure if Tessa got her own joke. "Is there anywhere else you can think of to have the auction and fashion show?" she asked.

"Not at this late date."

"*Che casino!*" Tessa said, switching into Italian. "I really thought we were going to pull off this event and then this happens!"

"HAT needs the money. You'd think Austin's wife would want to have the event in memory of her husband."

"Apparently Mrs. Greer doesn't see it that way. Her assistant, Nika, informed us a few minutes ago. We're all going home."

"Oh, I bet your girls are devastated."

"They are. All the girls are. So is Jaya."

"Maybe we can convince Mrs. Greer that it's still a worthwhile event, and that it's a way to carry on Austin's legacy. Wait a minute—I have an appointment to see Amanda Greer tomorrow. She wanted to see my beads."

"That's great, maybe you could convince her to let us keep going and delay shutting down the theater."

"I don't know, a lot has changed for her since we set up the appointment. She may not even want to have me visit. I'll get in touch with her assistant and see if Mrs. Greer still wants me to come."

Tessa wished me good luck and we ended our call.

I texted Nika to confirm that Amanda still wanted me to come over with my beads. Minutes later, my phone pinged, and I had a message confirming Amanda Greer was expecting me the following morning at ten.

NINE

AS I DROVE the Ladybug through the posh neighborhood in the hills overlooking Lake Washington, I reflected on what it must be like to live on a street like this, with perfectly landscaped lawns, wide driveways, and lake views.

The Greer house was much like many of the other mansions in the area. Theirs was colonial. Its tall, pale columns flanked the front door and had no sense of warmth or hospitality. That and the gated entrance I'd had to pass through made me feel less than welcome. I parked in the curve of the circular driveway and hoisted my oversized tote from the trunk of my car. It contained everything I wanted to show Mrs. Greer today.

Nika answered the door. "Hi, Jax, so nice to see you again. Please come in."

"Thanks," I said, stepping inside. The foyer was vast—nearly the size of my living room. I wondered how anyone could keep such a huge house clean. Actually, I knew how they did it—they had staff. My only staff was Gumdrop, and he was pretty useless, except as an unwitting dust mop. I glanced up and saw a beautiful art glass chandelier. I recognized the style immediately—it had been made by Vega. I pushed away thoughts of a similar chandelier falling on

Austin just days ago and took a deep breath to calm my nerves.

"I'm so very sorry about Mr. Greer. His passing must have been hard on you and Mrs. Greer," I said.

"Thank you. Yes, this has been a trying time for the entire Greer family," Nika said. She was younger than me, in her thirties I guessed. I, on the other hand, was on my long, slow slide toward fifty. Nika was slender and had a professional air about her. With her cropped navy business jacket, matching slacks, and white scoop-necked silk shirt, she seemed like exactly the kind of person who would be a personal assistant for a wealthy couple. "Please come in. Mrs. Greer is expecting you."

The interior of the mansion was as ostentatious as the exterior. It made me realize that's just how Austin had been—ostentatious, or was that Austin-tatious? His arrogance didn't seem at all in sync with his volunteer work. Even though Austin Greer had been eccentric, he had also been a respected philanthropist by all accounts. I couldn't imagine who would have wanted him dead.

As we walked through the house, I wondered what it would be like to live in a mansion with a five-car garage, marble entry with clerestory windows, an expansive view of the lake, and elegant oriental rugs in hues of blues and greens—my favorite colors. Nika took me to an opulent study. The floor-to-ceiling windows, flanked with burgundy velvet draperies, let in gorgeous light on this sunny spring afternoon. Removing a crystal vase of flowers from a round cherrywood library table, she asked me if the spot would work for setting up my wares. I told her it was perfect.

"Would you like some coffee?" Nika asked.

"Oh, yes, I would love some, thanks—if it's not too much trouble."

"No problem at all," Nika said, gliding out the door.

I pulled a black velvet cloth from of my tote and spread it out across the small round table. Then I took out trays of beads and jewelry from my bag and arranged them. Nika returned with a silver coffee service for two while I organized my wares.

I had just finished setting up when Amanda Greer entered the study. She was a petite woman, her short hair artfully coiffed into a strawberry blonde pageboy. She wore a flowing multi-colored batik skirt with a wide belt, along with a vibrant red mandarin-collared blouse with an egg-sized silver pendant on a silk cord around her neck. It seemed out of scale for her slender frame, but somehow it worked for her.

"Hello. I'm Amanda," she said, giving my hand a dainty side-to-side handshake.

"Nice to meet you," I replied.

"Did you bring me some treasures?" she asked, clasping her hands together at her chest, dozens of silver bangles on her wrists clinking together as she did.

"I did. Oh, and my deepest sympathy for Austin's passing—he said you might like to see my glass beads."

"Thank you. Yes, yes, it's a hard time right now. So much to sort out, but you didn't come to hear about the dreadful death of my husband. Please show me what you have. I don't get out too often, so it's a treat to have a visitor come and bring me beautiful things, especially right now." She poured herself a coffee and offered one to me. I took the cup and thanked her.

"I brought some loose beads and some glass jewelry, too. I wasn't sure what you might be interested in," I said, picking up a set of three beads that all coordinated. "I made them in a torch with Italian glass. I've got a few different color combinations."

"Ah, they're delightful. As are these necklaces." She picked up one of the pieces. It was a set of matching turquoise glass beads with tiny flower and vine decorations, strung together on a satin cord. She turned to a large gilt-framed mirror hanging behind her and held the strand to her slender neck.

"What do you think? No, wait, let's ask Nika." Amanda pressed a small silver button on the wall by the light switch. Nika entered the room seconds later.

"What is it, Mrs. Greer?"

"I want you to look at this jewelry Jax brought. It's absolutely lovely," Amanda said.

"That's a pretty necklace," Nika said, pointing to the one Amanda was holding.

"I agree. I'd like to buy it. And which one would you like?" Amanda asked Nika.

"Oh, that's okay, you don't need to buy me anything," Nika said with a shake of her head.

"I insist."

Nika approached the table and looked at the pieces I had brought with me, while I stood back and sipped my coffee.

"I like this bracelet," Nika said, trying on a dark blue beaded cuff.

"Then it's yours," Amanda said. "Thank you, Jax, for bringing your beautiful things." Amanda smiled weakly. It was clear her husband's recent death had taken its toll. "I'd also like to order twenty loose beads for some new jewelry I'm creating, like these." She held out the necklace with the beads I had made in a frail hand.

"Of course, that would be wonderful. I can give you the wholesale price on those."

"Oh, no need, dear. We believe in supporting artists. You can work out the payment with Nika."

"Thank you. I'd love to see what you make with them," I said, as I packed up my things.

"Nika? That will be all. Thank you," Amanda said, and Nika hurried from the room.

"Austin told me you import beads from Thailand," I said as I busied myself loading the trays back into my tote.

"I do. Silver beads of all types. I keep them mostly for the jewelry I make, which I sell through some of the better catalogs—you know, Gump's, Metropolitan Museum, and such. Come, and I'll show you my warehouse."

Amanda and I walked through her home, which looked like a spread from Architectural Digest. She guided me through a set of French doors into her beautiful garden and through a breezeway that connected to a small building that appeared to be a converted carriage house. The inside was lined with tables covered in thousands of strands of Thai silver beads.

"Oh, my," I said, astounded by the sheer quantity of silver beads in all shapes and sizes heaped inside plastic bins on ten banquet-sized wooden tables.

"Yes, it is quite impressive," Amanda said with a smile. "Nika is doing a stupendous job running my mail-order business, but she needs a helper, poor thing."

It did seem like Nika had all sorts of jobs she did for the Greers. Nika walked among the tables pulling strands out of bins and checking them off a form attached to a clipboard as she filled an order.

"If you decide you want to buy any silver beads at all, please give Nika a call. She'll give you our best wholesale price. Now, I'm so sorry, but I have an associate coming over for a meeting, so I must dash. Nika—can you please show Jax the way out? And make sure she gets paid?"

It was now or never. I needed to ask Mrs. Greer about whether she would allow the theater to stay open so we could have our gala for HAT. I wouldn't get another opportunity, although I was nervous to ask, not knowing how she'd react. My throat was tight as I started to speak.

"Excuse me, Mrs. Greer, I heard you were closing the theater. We're planning an auction and fashion show for HAT—the Homeless Advocacy Team, that is. We don't want to cancel it. My friend Tessa and I are willing to make it happen, if you'll let us continue. The gala would bring in a lot of money for a good cause."

"Ah, I see. One thing you must realize about the Greer family is that we don't like to be in the spotlight. Austin, however, was an exception to the rule, if you will. The poor, dear man—just look what happened because of his foolishness."

"I don't understand."

"My dear, those of us with money, we can be targeted. I don't want to be paranoid, but there truly are people out to get us."

I had the sudden realization that Amanda Greer was not well. No wonder Austin had told me to come here. I didn't think Amanda would have ever left her house to visit my studio, or anywhere else, for that matter.

"Is that what you think happened? That someone killed Austin because of his wealth?"

"Of course it is. Serves him right for venturing out into the world, I'd say. That amazing chandelier—it just crashed to the ground. What are the chances it would hit Austin and not someone else?"

It was a good question, actually. According to Zachary, the support cables had been tampered with, but no one could be sure Austin had been the intended victim.

"HAT really needs the money. It sounds like there are a lot of really beneficial programs that won't get funded without the money they need to raise. And there are a lot of hardworking volunteers who are going to be disappointed if the event is canceled. HAT was important to Austin—I thought you might want to continue with the event in his memory."

"Jax, you have been so kind in coming today. How can I say no? Of course—carry on! Just don't plan on seeing me at the event. Nika, please call Daniel and have him get in touch with me about continued funding for the theater."

"Yes, ma'am," said Nika.

"Oh! And since it's an auction, I have a wonderful idea. How would you like a donation of an auction item?" Amanda asked.

"That would be terrific. We are a little short on jewelry for the models to wear ever since Frankie Lawton left and took his necklaces with him."

"Good riddance to bad rubbish. That's all I have to say about Frankie. So, now, let's see what we can find for you that would be truly spectacular." Amanda entered a small storeroom, which contained necklaces made from extra-large silver beads. "Now, I didn't make this necklace, but it was made by a wonderful designer in Thailand. I'm sure it will bring in top dollar."

Amanda handed the strand to Nika.

"Please wrap this up for Jax," she told her.

"I'm wondering if perhaps you'd like to donate something else. These are for a special order," Nika said, taking the necklace and attempting to put it back with the others.

"Oh, I'm sure we can let one go," Amanda said, placing her hand on top of Nika's and stopping her from returning the necklace to the shelf in the storeroom. Nika hesitated, then did as she was told.

TEN

AS I CROSSED the Greer's vast driveway, I got a call from Zachary.

"Hi. Did you get my message? I want to explain what you saw yesterday at my house. You see, that was my vet, well, actually—"

"Jax, can you slow down a minute? We need to talk." Zachary sounded serious, more serious than usual, which made me nervous.

"Perhaps you should take me out to lunch?" I said with a laugh, trying to lighten up the mood.

"Sure. Seafood? We could go to the new restaurant out in Ballard."

"Sounds divine. Pick me up at noon?"

"See you then. And Jax, I'm sorry I was so stern yesterday."

I nearly laughed, hearing him use the word I'd used so often to describe him. I was nervous about what Zachary wanted to talk with me about. Could this be a break-up lunch? I hoped not. I'd find out soon enough. In the meantime, I was going to have to practice my speech about why he'd found me half-undressed with a strange man drinking wine in my living room.

I spent the time before Zachary picked me up cleaning up around the house. I wasn't really a neat freak, but I did like things orderly, at least in the house. In the studio, it was another story. It was often in a state of moderately controlled chaos. I also took some time to get dressed for my lunch date. I wasn't sure what kind of date this was—perhaps it was even our last—but I didn't want to think about that. I slipped on a Val-approved lavender T-shirt. She approved of it because it hugged my curves nicely, more than many of the other baggy shirts I owned, and had a nice deep-V neckline. I slipped into my stretchy cropped black pants and put on a purple teardrop-shaped glass pendant on a short silver chain. I didn't think my lime green high top sneakers would be appropriate for the restaurant, so I slid on my favorite red leather clogs. Then I went to the bathroom to put on some makeup, what little of it I wore, and fixed up my hair with a little dab of styling wax Val had insisted I use.

Zachary picked me up as planned, and we headed toward the restaurant.

"So. I'm going to come right out and say what we need," he said, looking straight ahead as he drove. His sunglasses masked his eyes, giving me few hints about what was on his mind.

"'We?'"

"The department. You see, Jax, you've stumbled into something we've been trying to break open for over a year."

"Break open?" I breathed a sigh of relief. This wasn't about him breaking up with me, at least not yet.

"Yes, you see, there has been a suspicion for a long time that the Chanticleer Theater is some sort of a money laundering operation. As you can imagine, the murder of Austin Greer must be taken in the context of what else we know about his family and business. And, of course, it means this is more than just a homicide case."

I decided to wait for Zachary to say more, but he didn't. And I had no idea what to say. Driving in silence, we arrived at the marina a few minutes later. Being a gentleman, he opened the car door for me, and we walked together into the Neptuna Restaurant.

"Reservation for three," Zachary told the hostess.

"Three?" I asked.

"Jax, I invited you here because I want you to meet my partner for this investigation, Bev Marley," he said as we approached our table.

Bev Marley was pushing sixty years old, with brassy highlights on a well-lacquered helmet of hair and a black pantsuit that looked like it came from the clearance rack at Sears. She reached out and shook my hand with a ferocity commensurate with her solid stature.

"Officer Marley, but you can call me Bev. I'm from the Washington State Financial Crimes Unit," she said.

"Wait. I don't understand." I turned to Zachary. "Don't you usually want me to stay far, far away from your investigations? This seems like you actually want me to be involved."

"That's because we do, hon," Bev said. "I can't go sneaking around that theater. I would stick out like a sore thumb. And my boy Zee, here…" *My boy Zee?* I wanted to burst out laughing. "He's not much help; everyone gets real skittish when there's been a murder and he comes snooping around."

"And so you want me to do what, exactly?"

"We want you to find out where the Greers' money is coming from. What are they bringing into the state and selling—drugs? Girls? Weapons? And if they're bringing in money from some illicit source, how are they laundering it?"

I looked at Zachary for support.

"Jax, I have all the confidence in the world in you," Zachary said, taking my hand and giving it a smooch. Annoyed, I pulled my hand away from him. I was in no mood for him to sweet talk me into helping him when he'd spent so much time discouraging me in the past. Still, I was intrigued.

"What do you want me to do?" I asked again.

"We need you to get onto the computer systems at the theater— see if you can find their financial statements," Bev said.

"I can't believe you are actually asking me to help you. Isn't this dangerous?"

"We will always be close by," Zachary said.

"And here's the thing, hon," Bev said. "We're going to mic you up. That way if you get into trouble, we can get there, hopefully quick enough."

"*Hopefully* quick enough?" This whole thing was making me nervous. I felt like I was chum being thrown off the stern of a boat to lure in a great white shark.

Bev pulled a plastic bag out of her purse. It contained a small, cylindrical black microphone, about the size of my pinkie fingernail, attached to a thin cable and battery pack. She slid it across the table to me.

"This is the mic? Isn't it sort of obvious?" I asked.

"Sorry, we don't have anything else. Usually people just stick it in their cleavage if they can. Of course, that assumes you're wearing some sort of open neck blouse and have somewhere to hide the battery pack." She pushed the mic closer to me. I picked it up and put it in my purse. "Glad you're on our team."

"Do I have a choice?" I asked.

"Of course you have a choice," Bev said, "but from what I've heard from my boy Zee, you're a pretty good sleuth. I figured you would want to help us catch the bad guys."

"That's right. Jax has helped solve three other murder cases. Strictly speaking, she should have left it to the professionals, but she did some amazing work," Zachary said. I wanted to kick him under the table for saying I should have left the work to the professionals. Although it was nice to hear him say I'd done some amazing work in catching some murderers.

I'd been wanting to help. I just didn't realize I was going to have to catch bad guys while wearing a microphone and having police listen in on my every move. I had high hopes Zachary would come to appreciate my sleuthing skills if I was successful in helping on this case. It was a lot to wish for, but I was going to try my best to help Bev and Zachary.

"Now, Jax, hon. I want you to keep that mic on whenever you're going to be at the theater or the Greer residence, okay? You just act natural and try and find out what you can. This is not what you'd call our usual protocol, so I think you need to keep this on the down-low. Got it?"

"Gotcha."

A waitress appeared with a to-go bag and handed it to Bev. "I'm going to leave you two lovebirds alone. I've got my lunch here," Bev said, taking the bag of food and peeking inside.

We said our goodbyes to Bev, and Zachary opened his menu.

"Excuse me," I said, hooking my finger over the top edge of his menu and pulling it down. "So, is this Bev's case now?"

"No. I'm still working on the homicide aspect."

"Are you really considering the girls as suspects?"

"Unfortunately, yes, they remain under consideration, but some of the cast and crew members from *Hamlet* were at the theater after the models were, so I'm focusing on them as well."

"So the girls aren't in the clear?"

"No. Not yet. But we do have a clue from Austin that I'm working on, so you'll be relieved to hear Tessa's girls are no longer at the top of my person-of-interest list."

"What's that supposed to mean? He's sent a message from beyond the grave?" I asked.

"He tried to write a message as he lay dying after the chandelier fell, but we don't know what it means."

"How? What did he write?"

"He scraped the letters M and O into the stage floor with a broken piece of glass. So far, we haven't been able to determine who that might be. There are no teen models with those initials, nor any *Hamlet* cast members. For all we know, it could mean nothing."

"Seems to me it's not nothing—it would have taken a lot of effort to write those letters," I said, wracking my brain to come up with who or what MO could be.

"We're trying to determine if the suspect took Austin Greer's cell phone prior to killing him, to prevent him from contacting someone."

"I know for a fact Mr. Greer didn't carry a phone, but his assistant Nika did," I said.

"Yeah, Nika. We've not been able to uncover much about her so far. My team is working on it, but we've got more to do. But right now, I'm starving," Zachary said, opening his menu again, and holding my menu up for me. "Oh, and Jax, thank you." He leaned in and kissed me, which was surprising, and wonderful, since he wasn't always the best at public displays of affection. I did notice we were hiding behind tall menus, so perhaps we weren't so public after all.

The kiss was amazing, and it left me wanting more than just seafood for lunch. But what I really wanted was to know what Austin was trying to tell us in the message he'd left behind.

ELEVEN

AFTER LUNCH, Zachary brought me back to my house, and parked out front. As we came in the front door, we were back in the same spot where he had witnessed me just the day before running down the hall without a shirt on.

"About yesterday, I just want you to know that the man you saw here—"

"While you were half-undressed." Zachary had a bemused expression on his face, I was glad to see. I ignored him and carried on.

"That was Gumdrop's vet, Buff Brown." I said, as I headed to my studio to check on my cat.

"You have a vet who makes house calls? Impressive." Zachary followed me down the hall.

"Yes, and you should see the motorcycle he drives. It's really unique. He brought Gummie home to me in its sidecar." I found Gumdrop in his usual spot, sleeping in the sun on my worktable. He seemed like he was doing okay.

"He took your cat for a ride on his motorcycle? Now that is amazing. I'm surprised the man didn't end up sliced to ribbons from Gumdrop's claws."

"He has a special compartment, you'll just have to see it. Anyway,

I slipped and spilled wine on my shirt, and so I took it—"

"Hey, it's okay. I'm not mad. I had a little moment there, but I thought it was pretty funny when I thought about it. Besides, I didn't think he was your type."

"Oh, really? And what is my type?"

"Oh, I don't know. Someone like me?"

"Yeah, someone just like you." I smiled at him and pulled him into a hug.

"So, you're feeling okay about the microphone?" Zachary asked.

"I guess so. But, I was wondering, can we have a secret mayday word?"

"You mean something you can say to get us to come and rescue you? Sure, what do you want it to be?"

"Ice cream," I said.

"Ice cream? Okay, I'll make sure Bev is monitoring for those words. But you better stay out of any ice cream shops in the meantime. I wouldn't want the entire Seattle Police Department showing up because you went to Molly Moon's." Molly Moon's was my favorite ice cream shop in Seattle. I could never decide between strawberry balsamic and lavender honey. Darn, now I wanted ice cream.

I dug around in my purse trying to find the microphone Bev had given me. Instead, I found the business card I'd gotten from the owner of the boutique near the theater.

I gasped when I saw the name on the card: Cassie Morton.

"Here's something you need to check out," I said. "There's a boutique on the corner near the Chanticleer Theater, and the owner's name is Cassie Morton."

"That could be the MO we're looking for," Zachary said. "Then again, I don't think I can go around putting everyone whose name starts with MO on my person of interest list. Otherwise, I'd have to add Molly Moon to the list."

"I don't think Molly Moon is a real person," I said, as I continued pawing through my purse looking for the tiny listening device. "That's what I'm thinking."

I was also thinking how nice it was for Zachary and me to be working together. I'd spent so much time in the last year feeling like we were working against each other when it came to murder investigations. And this felt good, but I knew it wouldn't last.

I found the mic and handed it to him. "How does it work?"

"It's voice activated, so unless you're talking, all we'll hear is silence. Now, if you're talking with someone, and you want us to hear what they are saying, you don't need to get too close. This mic has a range of about twenty feet. Here's the power button, just press it once to turn it on, and press it again to power it off." Zachary showed me the little button on the side of the power pack.

"So, let me show you how to attach this mic somewhere discreet. It would be nice to see where you might tape it," he said, running his index finger gently, seductively, from my collarbone to my cleavage. Zachary had never been very good at talking sexy to me. He must've been improving, because I was definitely starting to feel flushed in all the wrong places—or maybe they were the right places.

"I'm really nervous about this little microphone. I'm worried about taping it to my body—what if I need to take it off? What if it comes unglued?" What if I became unglued was the real question, but I wasn't going to go there.

"You're going to be fine, and if you decide you don't want to do this, you just say the word. We want you to be comfortable." Zachary dropped his hand away from my chest.

"Could I just make a boutonnière out of it? You know, a pretty floral brooch. I could pin it to my jacket." I pulled the tiny listening device from its bag. It would be easy to camouflage. Hanging from the mic was a slender six-inch-long cable attached to a matchbox-sized battery case. "I can pin the hidden mic on the breast pocket of my denim jacket and pop the power pack inside the pocket."

"As long as you don't wreck the mic, I think it's okay for you to dress it up so it's undetectable," he said.

"Thanks. I'll feel more comfortable this way, and besides, I think it will be fun."

"In case you hadn't noticed, there's not much fun in homicide investigations," he said. "Although, you're my kind of fun." He nuzzled my neck and wrapped his arms around me. Having Zachary standing so close to me was giving me a serious heat wave, and I didn't mean the menopause kind. The sizzle stopped as soon as I heard my front door open and close gently. It had to be Val.

"Sorry, I'm going to have to take a rain check, okay? We're about to be interrupted," I said.

Zachary stepped away from me and straightened his tie. I reached over and smoothed out his hair.

"Jax?" It was Val, announcing her arrival more quietly than usual.

"Val! I'm back in my studio," I shouted.

"Shhhhh. Not. So. Loud. I'm a bit headache-y this morning," Val said as she entered my studio, looking bleary, wearing a pink satin robe and fluffy slippers that reminded me of pink versions of Gumdrop. "Oh, Zachary, I didn't know you were here. I hope I didn't...you know. Maybe I should be going."

"No, Val. You stay. I need to take off," Zachary said, heading for the door. We said our goodbyes, and Zachary whispered in my ear. "To be continued." I blushed ten shades of red, but I think Val was too hung-over to notice.

"I think I had a teensy-weensy bit too much to drink last night. That drinking game was a terrible idea. I think Rudy may have won. But I mean, what does it even mean to win that game?" Val asked.

"I don't know. Seems like you just call it a game because it's fun, not because you can win or lose. So, I guess that's the question: Did you have fun?"

"I did!" Val said, just a little too loudly for even herself. "I mean, I did, but ugh! I'm really regretting it today."

"And how's it going with the Werewolf Diet?"

"Pfft. I've given up on that one, I can't go all day with only liquids, even when there's vodka involved. I've moved on to the Sleeping Beauty Diet. That's why I just got up—that, and the hangover. And you, my little buttercup, how are you doing?"

"I'm okay. I've got a lot to do to get ready for the auction and fashion show Tessa and I are working on."

"Oh, a fashion show! Can I help? I adore fashion shows," Val said.

"As a matter of fact, I wanted to ask if you'd help with the hair and makeup for the models," I said.

"Say no more. Of course I will. Just tell me where and when, and I'll be there. As long as it's not sometime in the next few hours, because I think I'm officially indisposed for the rest of the day."

"I wish I could be indisposed, but I need to get back to work. I need to find jewelry for the outfits the models are wearing in the fashion show on Sunday.

"For the fashion show? Maybe you'd like some of my jewelry?" Val asked.

"Sorry, we need some things we can sell. You don't want to give up any of your necklaces, right?"

"Oh! You know, I think I have one for you. I'll find it and bring it over. It's from Luke, that *Awfulstralian*—"

"You mean awful Australian?"

"My brain's on the fritz today. But, yes, exactly. You remember Luke, who gave me that necklace at the bead bazaar? It gives me bad memories. Can I donate it?" Luke, an Aussie we'd met at a bead bazaar in Portland last year, had given Val a super-sparkly necklace made of dichroic glass. He was quite a ladies' man, and wanted more than Val was willing to give, so I could see why Val might not have the fondest memories of that necklace.

"That would be terrific. Now all I need is a new emcee to replace Frankie Lawton, who bailed out on us. Do you think your Uncle Freddie would do it?"

"Sorry, honey bunny, he's on tour right now. I don't even know where we'd find him—probably in some giant stadium playing with his band." Val's uncle had recently moved to the town of Carthage, about a forty-five-minute drive from here. He was in the process of buying and renovating a café so he could create a rock n' roll restaurant. I'd gotten to know him last month when he was hiding out at Val's house while looking for a property to purchase.

"Dammit! He was my only hope for an emcee." It certainly wasn't going to be me. While I was okay talking in front of small groups of people, I didn't think I could handle standing up on the stage at the Chanticleer Theater running the show, let alone trying to be an auctioneer.

"If I think of someone, I'll let you know. I'm going to go and make some coffee, take a couple of aspirin, and try to recover. Remind me never, ever, ever to play that silly game again. I'll bring the necklace over later, okay? I think I need to go lie down," Val said as she shambled out the door. She clearly wasn't feeling well enough to sashay.

I sat at the worktable in my studio, selecting beads and using wire to wrap the mic and make it into a festive floral boutonnière. I was amazed Bev and Zachary even considered giving me a mic and were willing to let me work on the case. I'd gone from being a source of derision for Zachary to actually helping on an investigation, and that felt good. He and Bev had warned me about how dangerous this could be, but, really, how bad could it be, if they were always listening? The police could send someone in to rescue me if things got too crazy. I hoped that was true.

After I finished decorating the microphone with a cute cluster of glass flowers, I glued a pin-back onto it. Then I moved on to my next project: organizing the jewelry I'd gathered so far for the event. I laid out the two necklaces I was donating, and next to them I placed the Thai silver necklace Mrs. Greer had given me. Then I found the faux amber necklace Mr. Chu had given me, and placed it next to the others. Once I added Val's piece, I would be half-way finished with my necklace treasure hunt. I had more hunting to do and knew where I needed to go next.

By the time I was ready to go, the glue on my newly camouflaged microphone was dry. I brought my favorite denim jacket into the studio and pinned the brooch to its front pocket. Then I pressed the button on the microphone to turn it on, slid the batteries into the pocket, and pulled on my the jacket. I grabbed my handbag and headed out the door.

"Testing, one, two, three," I said to the flowers pinned to my jacket. Seconds later my phone rang.

"Yeah, we hear ya, hon. Loud and clear," Bev said.

"Do I really have to have this on all the time?" I asked.

"Let's just consider this a test run. You just go about your business, and we'll see how it goes. My boy Zee called me and told me about your clever camouflage job. Hope that works for ya."

"Bev? Why do you call Zachary 'my boy Zee?'"

"Ah, it's just a joke, really. Seems like I've known him since he first started on the force, before I moved to my new role with Washington State."

"And why doesn't he like it?"

"Because he's too damn serious. Haven't ya noticed that, hon?" Bev cackled and hung up.

My first stop was Tessa's studio. I wanted to ask Tessa's assistant, Dylan, if he would be willing to donate a necklace to the fashion show. He was working at a torch making a bead in the back of the shop when I arrived.

"Hey, Jax. I'll be done in a minute," Dylan said when he spotted me coming in the door.

"Take your time," I said, settling in to watch him work. He was already a terrific beadmaker at the tender age of twenty-three. I wondered what his work would be like by the time he was my age. He'd probably be phenomenal given how talented he was already. Dylan worked in a different kind of glass than Tessa and I did. While we worked in Italian glass, which was excellent for making beads, Dylan worked with borosilicate glass that was popular for making hollow blown forms. Borosilicate glass was favored by some of the younger men we knew, who we called *boro boys*. And Dylan, who reminded me of a surfer dude with his shaggy blond hair, jeans, and flip-flops, was one of them, although he tended to make hollow beads rather than pipes. And it wasn't just the boro boys who had a special moniker. We were called *bead ladies*.

"You're not looking for Tessa, are you?" Dylan asked.

"No, actually, I'm looking for you. I'm wondering if you might be interested in donating a necklace to the charity auction she and I are working on. I can pay you half of whatever it sells for."

"That would be cool. Look in that bag over there on the counter.

There are a few necklaces in there you can choose from," Dylan said, sliding his completed bead into the kiln on the workbench. "I just got them back from a boutique over near Yesler Square."

I pulled a box out of the bag and opened it. Then I opened another, and another. Each necklace was more exquisite than the last.

"Dylan, these are magnificent," I said, laying three necklaces out on the counter. "How can I possibly choose?" Each was made of five glass disk-shaped beads, with each disk a swirl of two colors. All the discs were slightly different, but all coordinated. The first was olive and burgundy, the second was lime and cobalt, and the third was black and white. The label on the outside of the shopping bag I'd pulled the necklaces from read: Styles by Cassie.

"Was your work at a little store near the Chanticleer Theater?" I asked Dylan.

"Yeah, the owner was nice, but she told me she was closing her shop and wanted me to take my inventory home. Too bad, too, because she had sold a lot of nice pieces for me." That was strange. Dylan must have been the jewelry designer Cassie said hadn't worked out. I wondered why she'd told Dylan she was closing and told me something else. There were no signs in the window saying she was going out of business, and she hadn't mentioned it when I was speaking with her. Come to think of it, she'd been supervising someone installing security gates on the shop's windows when I passed by. I wouldn't think she'd be adding new equipment to a property she was just about to leave. I wasn't sure what it meant, but in light of the MO clue, I had to wonder even more what motive Cassie Morton might have for the murder of Austin Greer. I was going to need to tell Zachary or look into this myself.

I refocused my attention on Dylan's fabulous necklaces and thought about the outfits I still needed necklaces for. "Oh, it's so hard to choose! I think I want the black and white set." I wasn't certain which outfit I'd put this necklace with, but since it was neutral, it could coordinate with just about anything, and it was stunning.

"Yeah, no problem. That's a pretty one. What's it for?"

"A fundraiser for the Homeless Advocacy Team. They help teens and young adults find housing and jobs."

"That's cool. I know lots of people who need support to get their lives back together. I could've used help like that a few years back," Dylan said.

"Speaking of help, do you have any extra time tomorrow when you could help me move some stuff out of my attic? I'm getting ready to renovate it."

"Sure. I'll come over around nine, okay?" Dylan placed the necklace in a box, tied a ribbon around it, and passed it to me. I had one more necklace to add to my collection for the auction.

"Nine sounds great. I'll pay you and feed you."

"That's cool, Jax, you've helped me plenty. I'm happy to do it."

"I'm still going to pay you." I wanted to help Dylan. He was a good guy and was trying his best to become a responsible member of society. He and his girlfriend, Tracy, and their little boy, Benny, had become a family, and that was wonderful to see. Even though they were still young, they seemed to be trying hard to work on creating a positive and supportive environment in which to raise their son.

I noticed a box on the counter addressed to Vega.

"Sorry to be nosy, but are you shipping this box out to Vega?"

"Yeah, she ordered some glass. I've got to get it to the post office, either that or borrow Tracy's car and deliver it to Vega's studio. Seems sort of silly to mail it, since her studio is just a few miles from here," Dylan said.

"You know, I need to go see Vega anyway. Would you like me to take it to her?" I asked.

"I don't think Tessa would mind. It would save money on postage, and save me a trip to deliver it."

"No problem," I said, grabbing the box for Vega, as well as the box with Dylan's donated necklace in it.

Vega's workshop was near another studio I had visited recently, that of Duke Kaminski, a student in the glassblowing class I'd taken a few weeks ago out in Carthage. My experiences during that workshop had convinced me I should stick with making glass beads and not attempt to work on large-scale glassblowing projects.

The entrance to Vega's studio was a sliding door made of rusty, banged up corrugated metal mounted on two crooked rails. It was padlocked with a sign in the middle of the door that had the word PRIVATE neatly lettered in felt-tip pen. I put my ear to the door. Inside I could hear loud rock music, along with the roar of the glassblowing equipment and the occasional clank of metal on metal. Vega—or someone—was working in the studio. Since the lock was on the outside of the door, whoever was in there couldn't have locked themselves in. I knew there must be another entrance, so I walked along the side the building, turned the corner, and slid into a passageway that was a mere three feet wide. When I got to the corner I took another left, which opened up into a quad that led to the open doors of Vega's studio.

Vega was busy at the glory hole, a bucket of fire on its side, reheating a glowing glass sphere. She was the woman with the shaved head whom I'd noticed sitting in the theater a few days ago.

I stood well back from her and made some throat-clearing noises so I wouldn't startle her. The rock music was so loud, I was pretty sure she couldn't hear me. She pulled the orb from the glory hole and took a seat at the glassblower's bench, then shaped the hot glass into a cylinder with a piece of wet newspaper, which was the only thing protecting her bare hand from the molten mass. Steam rose from the piece as she worked. She didn't look up, but at this point, she must have seen me.

"What can I do you for?" Vega asked, finally looking my way. "I don't get too many visitors here—that's why there's a padlock on the front door. It discourages people like you."

"I brought you a package from Fremont Fire. I was over there, and I saw it on the counter, so I decided to bring it by. I also wanted to talk to you about possibly making something for me."

"Well, just hang on a minute, until I get this piece done." She used the jacks, a set of long, heavy-duty tweezers, to mark the location where she wanted to remove the piece from the punty, or handle, that she was working on. Then she squeezed a little water into the crease she made in the glass with the jacks.

Vega took the punty, with the vase still on the end of it, over to a tray covered in a heat-resistant blanket, and gently tapped on the punty with her tweezers. The piece dropped silently onto the fireproof fibers, unharmed. She slipped on some enormous heat-resistant mittens, picked up the vase and hustled to the kiln. Using a foot pedal and a series of pulleys, she opened its door and gingerly placed the vase inside. Then, tapping the foot pedal again, she swung the kiln doors shut. As I looked around her studio, I realized she had reworked the entire space to make it possible for her to blow glass by herself. She'd installed cables, pulleys, and clamps that allowed her to do solo the things that typically required two people working in tandem.

Vega picked up a water bottle from the table next to where I was standing and took a long swig.

"Thanks for dropping off the box. Anything else you need? Otherwise, I've got to get back to work." Vega was clearly not someone who believed in idle chit-chat.

"I'm interested in buying one of your light fixtures for an attic renovation. Do you have anything small that might work on the ceiling of a converted attic?"

"I've got a lot of small domes that might work for you. I can easily make them into fixtures. Let's take a look." Vega took me into her storage room and showed me the shelves full of glass domes in every color imaginable. There were combinations of three or more colors in each piece. One had a mix of red, green, and orange, another was purple, magenta, and blue. Each one seemed more beautiful than the last, and there were just too many to choose from. I couldn't figure out which one to choose—I wanted them all, but I knew that wasn't an option. When I got to the end of the shelf, I went back to the beginning of the row and picked up the second glass dome I had seen and forced myself to make a decision.

"I'd like this one, please," I said, handing Vega a dome with purple, magenta, and blue glass. I thought it might go well with the pale lavender I was planning for the wall color in my renovated attic.

"It has all my favorite glass colors in it."

"Are you a glass artist?"

"Yeah, a beadmaker," I said, feeling a little embarrassed. I couldn't make anything as large and fabulous as she did. I was just getting ready to say as much when she broke into my thoughts.

"Ah, Lord, I wish I could make beads. Everything is too tiny. How do you make all those miniature things?"

"I don't know, practice, I guess. Beadmaking is just like what you do, really. We have all the same moves, just on different scales. You roll your work across a three-foot marver," I said, referring to the steel table where glass artists shape their pieces. "I marver on something three inches long instead." I was glad she didn't think that just because I created small things that my work was unimportant or didn't stack up to the impressive sculptures and vessels glassblowers can make.

"Are you going to the fashion show at the Chanticleer Theater? It looked like some of Frankie Lawton's jewelry was going to be auctioned off at some event this weekend."

"Yes, as a matter of fact, I've been working on the event. But things have sort of fallen apart," I said.

"What do you mean?"

"You don't know?" I'd assumed someone had called and told her that her exquisite chandelier was destroyed. "Ah, geez, well, your chandelier fell…"

"Fell? That's not possible. I hung that chandelier myself. There is simply no way it could have fallen unless someone had tampered with it."

"I'm sorry to say that when it fell…"

"Yes, right, I can imagine, it broke into a million pieces." Vega grabbed a hand towel and wiped her face and bald head.

"Yes, and when it fell, it killed someone."

"Ah, crap! No. That's the worst. What happened? Who died? Do they know if it was an accident? Those cables wouldn't spontaneously release. I designed that system, so there was no way for it to fail." She threw the towel down on the table and started pacing maniacally in front of me.

"The police are looking into what happened. But Austin—"

"Austin? Austin Greer is dead?"

"I'm afraid so."

Vega let loose a sickening high-pitched squeal of grief.

"I'm so sorry I upset you. Did you know him well?"

Her squeals turned into sobs, and she dropped into a nearby chair.

"I was his daughter, that is, until he disowned me, and replaced me with that vile Nika girl. The last time I saw him, I told him I was looking forward to the day he died."

TWELVE

"WHY DID YOU DO THAT?" I asked, shocked on all sorts of levels.

"We were arguing. He kicked me out."

"You're Amanda and Austin's daughter?"

"I'm afraid so, though these days, I'm assuming they don't really like to admit they have a daughter. Especially a daughter who looks like this."

"What do you mean?"

"My body art. He's never understood why I love tattoos and piercings so much. If he'd ever gotten one, maybe he'd understand." Both of Vega's arms were covered with tattoos from her wrists to the edge of her t-shirt. That was all I could see, but I expected there were many more. Combined with her shaved head and multiple nose, eyebrow, and large-gauge ear piercings, she was one of the edgiest looking people I'd ever seen.

"I'm sure your dad loved you regardless," I said.

"Don't call him my dad. He was never much of a father."

"Okay, Austin, then. He must've have cared about you. You two had a disagreement; he didn't like some of the choices you made…"

"You know, Austin offered to pay to get my tattoos removed. He was so generous," she said with a sarcastic smirk, "he said he'd pay for removing them to make me beautiful again. He even tried to line up a cosmetic surgeon. He wanted to make me look socially acceptable—for the first time since I was a child. Of course, he could try to 'fix' me, but he couldn't understand me."

"Maybe he just wanted you to be happy. Maybe he felt guilty about something that had happened between you two and was trying to make things better."

"Obviously, you didn't know him well. I don't think he ever felt guilt a single day in his life."

Could Vega have killed her father? I was starting to think so. She was at the theater the night Austin died, so it was possible she had been able to drop the chandelier on him. She certainly knew how to release its cable and safety chain. But why would she destroy her own artwork just to watch him die? Maybe there was some poetic justice in that—killing Austin with the work she loved. But her reaction right now, unless she was a superb actress, was real. She truly was upset to hear her father had been killed.

"Believe me, between him and my mother, it was not what you'd call an ideal childhood."

"I met your mother. She seemed nice, maybe a little eccentric."

"'A little eccentric?' Try a lot. Anytime she felt threatened, and that was often, she'd retreat to the panic room, and I might not see her for hours. Austin wasn't always the gentlest guy, to add to his list of unappealing characteristics. Luckily I had a responsible nanny to take care of me," Vega said, pulling out plastic containers full of colored glass powders from the shelves as she prepared to blow another vase.

"I'm truly sorry." I couldn't think of what else to say.

"Don't pity me. I'm actually doing fine. I love working by myself. I love being on my own, though sleeping in the loft above the furnace isn't that pleasant. I never get cold, though."

"How about your mother? Do you see her?"

"Not since Austin and I had our falling out. And she'd never come here to reach out to me. You must know she never leaves the house.

The agoraphobia has gotten pretty severe in recent years, but she won't seek treatment, so she makes the world come to her."

"I saw you at the theater the other night," I said, trying to sound as casual as possible, so she didn't feel I was threatening or accusing her. "Why were you there?"

"I stopped by to see if I could patch things up with my father, but he was too busy being Saint Austin to take much time out to talk with me. He felt so righteous with that chandelier hanging above our heads."

"Did you donate the chandelier to him?"

"Donate? I didn't donate it. He paid me for it. I was happy to sell it, and believe me, he didn't get the friends and family discount."

"He paid you for the chandelier and then turned around and donated it to the auction?"

"Look, I don't know what he did with it after he bought it. Or why he would even do that. Sounds crazy to me. Of course, that would sum up my father."

I wondered if Austin buying expensive things and donating them to the theater, or to nonprofits like HAT, played into the money laundering scheme Bev Marley was trying to uncover. I didn't know much about money laundering, except that it had something to do with moving cash around to make it look like it didn't come from an illegal source. I still had no idea what the source could be.

"I'm sorry to have taken up so much of your time, and I'm sorry to be the one to deliver such tragic news." I pulled my credit card out and offered it to her. "Do you want a deposit for the light fixture you're making me?"

"No, it's okay. But, when it's ready, you should know I only accept cash. Yeah, I even made Austin pay cash. Of course, that's how he prefers it."

"I hope you don't mind me asking—how much does a chandelier like the one Austin bought cost?"

"A cool twenty grand." Vega grabbed her blow pipe from a bucket of water and gave it a little puff of air to clear the water from it.

"Wow. Congratulations on that. Wouldn't that give you enough money to live somewhere other than here?" I looked around at her studio, it was pretty rustic, to put it mildly.

"When you consider the number of months it took to make that chandelier, it's really not that much." She adjusted the tools on her work bench, putting them in a specific place so she could automatically grab them without searching when she needed them.

I could relate. After I paid my bills, all the money I'd made on my art never seemed to add up to much. But I understood why she did it. The desire to make art was powerful.

• • •

As I walked back to my car, I got a call from Bev. I put her on speaker phone as I drove away from Vega's studio.

"Where were you? I couldn't hear a thing," she said.

"I was in a glassblowing studio. It was pretty loud in there. I didn't have any control over that." Between the music, the exhaust system humming above our heads, and the roar of the glory hole, I could understand why all that noise would interfere with the microphone.

"Did you learn anything of interest?" Bev asked.

"Turns out the glassblower I was visiting is Austin Greer's daughter," I said.

"We've done a little background check and had discovered he had a daughter—Vivian Greer, but we hadn't been able to locate her. How'd you find her?"

"I showed up at her studio, but I didn't know she was his daughter until she told me. She goes by the name Vega now, just Vega—no last name, so I didn't know she was related. She didn't know her father had been killed, and she was pretty freaked out to hear the news."

"Good work, hon. I'll make sure to follow up on her. She doesn't seem to have been part of the picture with the family's finances, so that may be a dead end, but we'll check it out," Bev said.

"I'm not sure how this fits in, but it sounds like Austin spent a lot of money on the chandelier and then turned around and donated it to HAT. And get this, he paid for it in cash. According to his daughter, he paid for everything in cash."

"Interesting. I'm not sure how that fits into the larger scheme we're looking at, but it's certainly odd behavior. Who'd he buy it from?"

"What's weird is he bought it from his daughter, who, from what I understand, had been disowned by her father," I said.

"Other than the fact he had just bought an outrageously expensive chandelier from her," Bev said.

"Right, except for that." I turned on to I-5, heading north. "Maybe she's not involved in the money laundering, but she still could be the killer, right?"

"When you've been in the business as long as I have, you get a sixth sense about this stuff. I think Austin Greer died because of his financial dealings, and whoever killed him had a lot to gain."

"But she's his daughter, wouldn't she gain something from the inheritance?" I asked.

"Not necessarily. First, Mrs. Greer is still alive so any estate funds would go to her. Second, if he disowned her—or vice versa—she may have been cut out of whatever estate plans he'd made."

Vega certainly was on my list of suspects. Whether she was on anyone else's remained to be seen.

"Now, what we really need is for you to get into the theater and see if you can get into the filing cabinet, or get onto the computer in the office to see what you can find in the way of bank statements, or if there is a safe, see what's inside. You're looking for large quantities of cash or contraband."

"Right, I'll just find the safe hanging open if I'm lucky," I said, feeling like this was going to be fruitless and could get me in big trouble if I were caught.

"It's a long shot, I know, but I have faith you'll be able to find something."

"I'll let you know what I find out."

"I'll be listening," Bev said.

I hung up with Bev and called Zachary.

"Grant," he said, picking up the phone. He always sounded so stern until he realized it was me.

"Is everything okay? You sound..."

"Tired? Yes. I'm going through some recent toxicology reports. I am tired—sick and tired—of getting results like this. Another drug overdose. Hold on. This is the toxicology report for Austin Greer. Wow—he had enough narcotics in his system to kill a horse—or a dinosaur," Zachary said.

"Dinosaurs are already dead—" I said, trying my best to lighten the mood. Zachary ignored my comment.

"It looks like Austin had high levels of opioids in his system when he died. He might have had some chronic pain, or maybe he'd had some surgery that required painkillers that he'd never been able to get off of."

"Were they prescription drugs? Could he have been using drugs he bought on the street? Knowing that could point us—I mean you—to the killer."

"The medical examiner, when she's doing these quick tests, can only check opioid levels. For more specific tests that can identify the more refined types of chemicals, she has to send them out to the state lab. Those results can take weeks, even if she requests for them to be processed quickly."

"So all we know was he was high on something when the chandelier crushed him. We don't know what, and we don't know why." Was it possible someone was trying to kill Mr. Greer with drugs, got tired of waiting, and simply took a faster, and more gruesome, route that led to his demise?

"Were you listening a little while ago? Did you hear what I said about Vega being the Greers' daughter?"

"I heard you tell Bev, but couldn't hear a thing wherever you were before that."

"I was in a glassblowing studio. It was kind of loud in there. Don't you think the fact she's Austin's daughter makes her a prime suspect in his murder? She knew how to disable the safety system on the chandelier, she was in the theater the night Austin died, and she had a reason to kill him," I said.

"Yes, I'll need to look into her. She certainly seems like she's got some issues that need explaining. Good job, Jax."

My phone beeped in my ear. I had another call coming in. "Oh, sorry! I've got another call. Gotta run." I hung up on Zachary and picked up for Tessa.

"So, did we get approval to continue? I'm at the theater, and I'm not sure if I should turn everyone away. We've already got a crowd here wondering whether we should even bother to rehearse."

"Amanda told me we could go ahead with the event."

"That's a relief! Now the girls can stop sulking and start worrying about whether they're going to get dragged off to the police station to be questioned about Austin's murder, or worse," Tessa said.

"Look, we know the girls are innocent. We just have to make sure the police are looking at other suspects—and I'm finding plenty. On top of that, Zachary just told me Austin had drugs in his system when he died."

"I thought he died from the chandelier—"

"He did, but the drugs could mean he was killed for reasons other than being mean to a few high school girls."

"I'm glad to hear it. Meanwhile, you better get over here. The cast of *Hamlet* just arrived, and I don't think they're supposed to be here. Austin told us weeks ago we could use the stage right now."

"But Austin's not around anymore to confirm that."

Tessa muttered something in Italian and hung up.

As I drove to the theater, I thought about the opioids in Austin's system. If he'd had an accident or physical ailment that required drugs, that might be a clue to what happened to him. If street drugs were involved, perhaps Zachary would need to look at a wider circle of suspects or accomplices. If we weren't going to be able to find out more about the opioids for several weeks, though, I'd have to resort to other sources of information. And I just happened to know someone who could help me.

"Hey you two," I said to Bev and Zachary who were no doubt listening. "I'm going to switch off my mic to make a personal call." Then I pressed the power button on the tiny mic on my jacket. I wasn't sure how they might react to my not-strictly-speaking legal methods of obtaining information.

I called my brother Andy.

"Hey there," Andy said when he answered my call. "Let me guess. You need a little digital undercover work to find something out."

"How did you know?"

"Because you never call me except for that."

"Sorry." I made a silent promise to myself to call my brother more often.

"I'm just messing with you. It's really my pleasure. Way more interesting than fixing bugs, which is my task for this afternoon." My brother lived in San Francisco and was the founder of an Internet security start-up called Pook. While he was paid well, and his apartment was lavish, most of his job involved a lot of sitting and staring at a computer screen. I couldn't think of anything I would like less than sitting at a desk day after day. That's why I'd left my corporate job a few years back and became a full-time artist.

"I'm wondering if you can find out about a man who had a lot of drugs in his system at the time of his death."

"Did he die of an overdose?"

"No, that's the weird thing. He died when a chandelier fell on him."

"How awful! What a way to go," Andy said.

"I think it's important to find out whether the drugs were street drugs or prescription. I think it will help us narrow down the potential suspects. For instance—if he was injecting himself with heroin he bought on the street, we might need to look at a drug dealer as a suspect. Or, he could have been getting prescription drugs from any number of illegal sources."

"I don't know, Jax, you're asking for a lot. Look, it used to be pretty easy to hack into medical records—lots of systems were breached. But these days, the hospitals and doctors have been really locking things down. I'll see what I can do, but no promises."

"Hey, I appreciate anything you can find out, little bro."

"I live to serve," Andy said with a chuckle. "Besides, I could use a break from staring at all of this programming code. What am I looking for?"

"We're looking for some evidence that Austin Greer took painkillers—you know, any of the opium-based drugs. See if you can find out if he's had any recent surgeries or seen any pain management doctors," I said.

"Okay, but I wouldn't plan on any miracles. Give me a day or two."

Pulling into the parking lot at the Chanticleer Theater, I said goodbye to my brother. The police had finally cleared away the crime scene tape and packed up, I was relieved to see as I entered the backstage area.

I wandered to the center of the stage and realized I was standing on the very spot where Austin had died. A shiver ran down my spine. I looked up to the grid where the chandelier had once hung. What a shame it had been destroyed, but even more so that a life had been lost.

I looked down at the stage floor. It was nicked and dented. It was likely many of those flaws had occurred over time, and not all at once with the drop of an art glass lighting fixture, but it still gave me the creeps. The stage was newly repainted, covering up the scrapes and bloodstains from when the chandelier had crashed down on Austin. I noticed there were still some deep gashes a few feet from where I stood. Bending down, I examined them. The gashes formed the letters: MO. They'd been painted over but were still visible. Austin's incomplete message was as puzzling as ever. It gave me a queasy feeling in the pit of my stomach, thinking about how he struggled to write those letters during his final moments.

I couldn't find Tessa in the wings, so I wandered out to the lobby to see if I might find her there. I found Daniel in the box office, sitting behind a small ornate desk that must have been used in a theatrical production in the past, because it didn't look like something you'd use in a modern office. The desk was piled with papers and various strange items: fake mustaches, baby shoes, and an artificial houseplant that had seen better days. Daniel was typing away at top-speed on a beat-up laptop. He paused and looked up at me as I entered.

"Hi, Daniel. How are you doing?" I asked.

"Oh, I'm okay. It's just hard right now. I keep thinking about Austin. We'd had a little disagreement, and it's just sad. We never got a chance to talk again under better circumstances before he passed." Daniel covered his eyes, trying to hide his tears. "And to think he was murdered. Such a shame."

"I saw you arguing with him and Frankie Lawton the night he died. Is that what you mean?"

"Oh, that was just Frankie being his usual demanding self. It got a little heated, I'm sorry to say. I never got a chance to catch up with Austin after that and talk with him. I just regret our last words were angry ones."

"Any idea who'd do such a thing?" I figured I'd ask, though I didn't expect much from Daniel.

"Amanda was sure someone was out to get him."

"Can that really be true?" I asked.

"He had enemies. I never knew why. It seemed to me he was such a giving person, always doing charitable work in the community. Making donations to nonprofits like the Homeless Advocacy Team." Daniel's voice cracked, just a little. "Even though that Jaya woman never seemed to appreciate it."

"I'm so sorry. This must be really hard for you. Maybe you should take some time off. Do you want me to help out here while you take a break?" I did have an ulterior motive for making this suggestion. After all, if Daniel were gone, I'd have more of an opportunity to search his office for signs of financial misdeeds and reasons for murder.

"No, no. I'm fine." Daniel gave his cheeks a little pat, a futile attempt to perk himself up.

There was a two-drawer metal filing cabinet that looked promising, but no safe, at least that I could see. It would be good to search the drawers and get a peek in that laptop, but that wasn't going to be possible while Daniel was present. I was going to have to get back in here when he wasn't around. But when?

I took my leave of Daniel and headed back into the theater in search of Tessa. I checked the dressing room, and was surprised to run into Ryan Shaw. He was a hunky security guard I'd met last year in Portland and had almost had a fling with. He'd moved to Seattle to join the police department. I'd hoped he and I would get together at least occasionally, because he had major boyfriend potential. In the end, it hadn't worked out, when he started stalking me a little more than I thought was necessary. He'd lost his job with the police department over a stunt, which had saved me from a stint in the awful Carthage jail, when he pretended to be transferring me to another precinct for questioning. It was also an act of fraud that did not amuse the Sheriff of Carthage or Ryan's superiors in the Seattle Police Department. Ryan had taken a job working private security for Val's Uncle Freddie, but that didn't explain his appearance at the Chanticleer Theater.

"What are you doing here?" I asked, feeling a bit awkward about the unexpected run-in.

"I was going to ask you the same thing," Ryan replied. "I'm in a play that's going on here. It starts in just a few days."

"You're in *Hamlet*?"

"I *am* Hamlet."

THIRTEEN

WHEN I MET RYAN last fall, he told me he'd been an actor before becoming a security guard, but I was never sure if I believed him. He was handsome enough—tall with nice broad shoulders, full lips, close-cropped wavy hair, and brown eyes with flecks of amber. As I looked at him, I started to admire what a fine specimen of manhood he was. Then I remembered I already had a boyfriend. Zachary was an awesome guy, and he was not flaky, or a stalker, or an actor, for that matter.

"Congratulations on landing the lead role in the play," I said. It was impressive that he was the star of the show, and I gave him a congratulatory hug. Oh dear. This man was so well built, it was hard to let go. Ryan hugged me back and didn't seem to want to let go—or was that me? I finally broke away from him.

"Thanks. I'm glad I ran into you, Jax. Are you…seeing anyone right now?"

This was astounding to me. Ryan just never stopped. He simply couldn't understand how a woman wouldn't just fall at his feet. I was sure he'd had that happen to him his whole life, and he was confused as to why I wasn't one of them.

"Yes, as a matter of fact, I'm still seeing Zachary," I said.

"I just wondered if you two might want to come and see *Hamlet*. I could get you some tickets."

"Thanks, Ryan, I'll talk to Zachary and let you know." I looked up into Ryan's gorgeous brown eyes and wanted to melt in his arms.

Ryan had pulled his Hamlet costume from a rack nearby as we were talking, and I watched as he pulled his shirt off. I'd never actually seen him naked—even partially—before. His broad, muscular shoulders, six-pack abs, his slender hips—this man was an Adonis. I noticed my heart was beating extra fast. But, I had a boyfriend, and I needed to remember that, especially during moments like these. When he started to unbutton his jeans, I had to look away, not wanting to be tempted by his hot body. I didn't want to see him in his boxers, assuming he wore them. That might be just a little too much for my heart to take.

"I really should be going," I said, not knowing how much longer I could stay in the same room as Ryan without doing something I might regret later.

I did wonder though, if any of the cast or crew could possibly have had any reasons to want Austin dead, since, according to Zachary, some cast members had been in the theater the night Austin was killed.

I stopped in the doorway, not ready to leave, but not wanting to take a peek at Ryan. Finally I asked. "Um, are you decent yet?"

"I am now," he said.

I turned around to face Ryan, who was now buttoning up his fancy multi-colored duster. It looked like it had come straight from Boy George's wardrobe. Although it looked better on Ryan than it ever had on the 80s pop icon.

"Ryan? I know you're sort of out of police work at this point, but do you know if anyone in the cast or crew of *Hamlet* might have had an issue with Austin? You haven't heard anything about anyone here holding a grudge against him, have you?"

"Are you looking for a homicide suspect?"

"I think so, yes," I said. "But you didn't hear that from me."

"I'll see what I can find out, but really we just come in here and rehearse. I don't think any of us had much interaction with Austin. Our stage manager mostly talks with Daniel in the box office."

"Were you in the theater the night Austin died?"

"I was here with Leslie Dreyfus, our stage manager. We were rehearsing the scene with the ghost special effects. It didn't go well—the stupid ghost wasn't working right. We're going to try again today."

I suddenly remembered I had my mic pinned to my jacket, and was relieved when I remembered I'd turned it off when I called my brother. I decided to leave it that way. I was sure Zachary wouldn't approve, but what they didn't know wouldn't hurt them, I hoped.

"I'd like to do some snooping around. Do you think you could get me into the theater tonight after your rehearsal?" I asked in a low voice.

"I don't think that's the best idea. I broke some laws trying to protect you in the past, and I don't want to blow it again."

"It's not like we'd be breaking the law. We'd actually be helping with the investigation. You know who some of the suspects are? Tessa's daughters," I said, hoping he'd want to help if he knew Tessa's girls were in trouble.

"But they're just teens. They couldn't possibly have done it."

"Precisely. So, help me help them. And, I hate to mention it, but since you were in the theater the night Austin died, you're likely a suspect as well. Or at least a person of interest."

"Great. I can't wait to be interrogated by Zachary Grant. That'll be fun," Ryan said, with a resigned sigh. "Okay, I'll do it. But I'm only going to let you in—then you're on your own. I don't want to get thrown out of the cast of the show. Meet me here tonight at eleven," he said.

"Thanks. I'll see you tonight," I said.

"Why don't you stay for a while? We're going to run some cues for the ghost—it's pretty fun. You should watch."

I went and sat in one of the empty seats in the audience, hoping Tessa would eventually find me. Remembering, again, that I'd turned my microphone off when I called my brother, I pressed the power button on its power pack to turn it back on. I didn't want to leave it off for too long and risk Bev and Zachary getting mad at me for not using it. I watched as Ryan started his monologue while standing center stage. Leslie, seated in the glass booth overlooking the audience, spoke through the loudspeaker.

"Okay, ready in three, two, one," Leslie said. A ghostly gauze-draped figure swooped onto the stage from the wings, held aloft by thin cables. Ryan, as Hamlet, continued his monologue. Leslie's voice boomed from the loudspeaker. "Okay. Resetting. Next time, Ryan, you need to be farther stage left to be closer to the ghost."

Ryan started his monologue again. Leslie started her countdown for the ghost as Tessa dashed across the stage, joining Ryan center stage.

"Pause," shouted Leslie's disembodied voice. "Who the hell is that onstage?"

Tessa turned toward the booth. Shielding her eyes from the bright stage lights she said, "It's Tessa Ricci, with the fashion show and auction fundraiser. We need the stage."

"Sorry. We were told we could rehearse right now," Leslie said.

"By whom?" Tessa asked. I could see she was getting more and more perturbed by the second.

"Austin Greer. So you gals can just move along." Leslie's voice echoed through the theater.

Tessa mumbled something in Italian under her breath, probably a curse word. "But, he was working with us on the gala. He told me we could use the stage during the day for these few days before the event."

Leslie, her flannel shirt rolled up to expose some pretty impressive biceps, bolted from the booth and rushed toward the stage. "He's not here to ask, is he? So, unless you have some proof he told you that, I think you better be moving along."

Tessa pulled herself up to her full height, which reached five-foot-two on a good day. She refused to be bullied by this woman. Leslie reached the front row and stood glaring up at Tessa, furious. She adjusted her John Lennon style wire-rim glasses to get a better look at Tessa. For the first time in her life, Tessa towered over someone other than her children.

"I'm certain Daniel can confirm we have afternoons for rehearsing and you have evenings to rehearse *Macbeth*," Tessa said.

At the sound of the *Macbeth* both Leslie and Ryan gasped.

"What? What's wrong?" Tessa asked.

"Tessa, they're doing *Hamlet*, not *Macbeth*," I shouted from my seat.

Leslie and Ryan gasped again.

"You can't say the name of that play in a theater—it's cursed!" Leslie screeched and ran her hands through her short black hair.

"That's ridiculous," Tessa said as I applauded her sentiment from the audience.

"And you said it too!" Leslie whirled around to make eye contact with me. "You clearly don't understand that you never say the name of the Scottish play in a theater. It's bad luck. And now, unfortunately, you must fix it. Come with us."

Leslie grabbed Tessa by the arm, and Ryan grabbed my hand. They dragged us out into the back parking lot.

"What the heck is going on? Let go of me," Tessa said, yanking her arm away from Leslie. I was trying hard to not enjoy Ryan holding my hand with his big, strong, manly hand. But, finally, I resisted and released it.

"Now you've got to turn in a circle three times," Ryan told us as Leslie went back inside.

"You've got to be kidding," Tessa said as she started spinning.

"No, sorry, Tessa. But we've already had enough bad luck in this production without someone throwing the name of the Scottish play around."

"That's what you call that play—the Scottish play?" I said, starting to spin.

"We have to call it something, and it's terribly unlucky to say the real name," Ryan said, as he counted our spins. "Okay, now you have to spit on the ground."

We did as we were told but weren't happy about it. I'm not sure either of us had ever spit in public, at least not as adults.

"And then knock on the door to be let back in," Ryan said, ushering us to the door. Tessa knocked and I did too.

Leslie opened the door for us.

"Welcome back," she said. "Now that we've gotten that settled, what about the stage?"

"Well, I really do think we are supposed to be able to use it right now," Tessa said, continuing to hold her ground.

"Fine! You just do that. I don't get paid enough to deal with this B.S." Leslie stomped off while Ryan stood there not knowing what to do. Moments later, Leslie's angry voice burst through the sound system. "Rehearsal is over. Give the ladies the stage."

"Well, there you go. I guess you got what you wanted," Ryan said with a shrug.

"Why is Leslie so angry?" Tessa asked Ryan.

"Oh, just some bad blood between her and Daniel. I guess they both were up for the manager job here at the theater, and Austin gave it to Daniel. I guess she was upset with Austin about it, too. She's still working here, but only part-time. Her attitude has been pretty ugly for a while."

"Do you really need to rehearse?" I asked Ryan, feeling sorry for him.

"Yeah, we do. We've been having a lot of difficulties with special effects, and we haven't been able to use the stage while the theater was shut down when the crime scene crew was here."

I turned to Tessa. "Let's give them the stage. We're in okay shape for the event, aren't we?"

Tessa blew her bangs out of her eyes, a sure sign of her exasperation.

"Okay, you win. It's all yours, Ryan," Tessa said.

"Thank you, Tessa," he said with a bow, his Shakespearean character coming through. Ryan ran back to center stage. "Leslie? Let's continue, okay? Jax and Tessa are through for the day."

The disembodied voice of Leslie blasted through the speakers. "Fantastic. We've wasted enough time. Reset. Clear the stage."

Tessa rounded up the girls and stuffed them all into her minivan, and I took off in my car. I hoped Bev and Zachary had heard about the bad blood between Leslie, Austin, and Daniel—she was definitely someone to consider as a suspect in Austin's death. Whether there was enough of a problem to have pushed Leslie into a murderous rampage remained to be seen. One thing I did hope is that they didn't hear the whole kerfuffle about what I would forever more refer to as the Scottish Play.

FOURTEEN

WHEN I ARRIVED HOME, I found Buff Brown sitting on the front steps talking with Val. Now, this was an interesting development. Val's basset hound sat between them as they talked, his head bopping back and forth as he listened to each of them speak.

"Well, fancy seeing you here," I said to Buff, as I joined them on the stoop.

"I was in the neighborhood, so I thought I'd stop in and see how Gumdrop was doing. Oh, and I have some test results."

"It was super meeting you, Buff," Val said, a little more breathily than was absolutely necessary. She reached down and grabbed Stanley by the collar, giving Buff an extraordinary view of her cleavage. "I hope to see you again...soon."

"Why, yes, indeed, I hope so too," said Buff, blushing after having been exposed to Val's ample bosom.

"So, what can you tell me about Gumdrop? Is he going to be okay?" I asked as I led the veterinarian inside.

"Looks like Gumdrop has a virus. Has he been hanging around any other cats?"

"No. He's an inside cat. He has ventured outside before, but that was a year ago, and he hasn't done it since."

"It's a mystery, then. We'll keep an eye on him. He's getting to be an older cat, you know. You may start to see some signs of aging," Buff said.

I saw signs of aging in myself every day, so it was only natural that Gummie would be showing his age, too. I didn't like it one bit.

Buff picked up the whale carving I had left on the coffee table as a decoration.

"I've only ever seen one other of these. It's very rare, you know," Buff said, holding the tiny ivory sculpture in the palm of his hand.

"I was told it was valuable but not much more than that. What can you tell me about it?"

"I did some field studies in Northern Alaska a few years ago. The Inuit, an indigenous group commonly called Eskimo, carved walrus ivory and whalebone into all sorts of shapes, with whales being a common subject matter. Most of the small carvings were utilitarian, but some were made as trade goods. Where did you get it?"

"I found it inside a trunk that belonged to my great-aunt. How old do you think it is?"

"I'm not sure, maybe from the 1940s. That's when a lot of the trade for these small carvings started. This one is unusual, I think. See this little seam?" Buff pointed to a spot at the base of the tail. "This one may have a little compartment in it. Have you ever opened it?"

"No, I wouldn't want to break its tail off."

"Maybe you don't want to know what mystery lies within," Buff said with a mischievous gleam in his eye.

"I didn't realize it even had an inside. Funny, I often tell Val how important it is to look past the exterior of someone or something to see what lies inside, but usually we're talking about boyfriends."

Buff laughed, placed the carving back into my hands, and closed my fingers around it. I set it down on the kitchen counter, not wanting to think about what secrets the tiny whale carving might hold.

"I'm sure you'll figure out what you want to do with it. Now, where is that patient of mine?" Buff asked, looking around the house. We found Gumdrop sleeping in one of his favorite spots near the window in my studio. Buff spent a minute or two petting my cat, who perked up from all of the attention. Gummie seemed to be at least as smitten with Buff as Val was.

"Looks like Gumdrop is doing better. Just make sure he keeps drinking, and if anything changes, give me a call. Now, I really should be going," Buff said, walking back toward my front door. "Lots to do at my house. You don't know anybody who can do some home improvement projects? Like a painter?"

"As a matter of fact, I do. His name is Rudy—he's a friend of Val's," I said.

"A boyfriend?"

"No, she told me several times that their relationship is purely platonic."

"Oh, well, then..."

"In fact, I'll have her get in touch with you to give you Rudy's number."

"Can't you give me his number?"

"Of course I could, but then Val wouldn't have a reason to call you."

I closed the door behind Buff and smiled, feeling like such a clever matchmaker.

I tossed the jacket with the mic boutonnière on my bed. I needed to use the bathroom, and I didn't think Zachary and Bev would want to experience that in full-blown Dolby audio.

Zachary called. I was going to have to keep the conversation brief, because I didn't want to tell him I'd planned to go snooping at the theater in a matter of hours, or that Ryan was giving me access. Ryan and Zachary's mutual jealousy was something I'd experienced more than once, and it wasn't pleasant.

"You're not wearing your mic," he said.

"Sorry. I should be able to have a little privacy now and then, right? I'm home now. I struck out at the theater. Daniel seems to be a bit of a basket case. He was in the box office, so I couldn't do much searching for financial records for Bev."

"Thank you for trying. We'll figure out some other way. Don't worry about it. And if you start feeling uncomfortable about doing this work for us, just let me know, and we'll stop. I want you to be safe."

"I'm fine. I'm just glad I can help, though I don't feel like I've been all that useful—yet." I didn't want to tell him that I was going on a snooping mission tonight because I was certain he wouldn't approve. I changed the subject. If my sleuthing did turn up something tonight, I'd have to figure out a way to tell him, but I'd cross that bridge when, and if, I needed to.

"What happened to all the broken glass from the chandelier?"

"It's sitting in the evidence room taking up too much space—two Rubbermaid tubs of glass gravel. Actually, it's not all gravel. There are several good-sized spheres that survived the fall. If someone knew something about glass, they could make—" Zachary stopped talking. "No. Sorry. Forget I even said it. You cannot have the rubble from the chandelier."

"Please?"

"No. Seriously, those bins full of glass are evidence right now. When we're done with them, then maybe we can talk about it. Maybe."

"Okay, just know I have first dibs," I said, feeling not the least bit foolish for wanting buckets of art glass shards. I wasn't sure what I'd do with them, but I was certain I wanted them.

"Were you listening a little while ago?" I asked.

"You mean when you were talking with the vet? Yes. I was." Zachary said, his voice sounding warm, the way I liked it.

"He seems harmless, right?"

"I'm happy that he seems more interested in your cat than in you."

"Well, my boy Zee—"

"Do not call me that. Seriously. Not even Bev is supposed to call me that."

"Okay, don't get so uptight. I'll talk with you later," I said as I ended the call.

Gumdrop cruised into the room. I was glad to see him up and around. I brought him out to the kitchen and set him on the counter, as usual.

"Do you want something to eat?"

Gummie didn't say a word. He just stared at me with those big green eyes.

"Well, we can't let you waste away to nothing, can we? How about some tuna?" I fished out a can from the back of the pantry, opened it, and dumped it into a bowl. "Come on, big boy."

He took a few bites, which was progress. Then he wandered over to the whale carving, which I had left on the counter, and gave it a swat.

"Gumdrop! You naughty boy!" I said, grabbing the carving. Not liking to be yelled at, he jumped off the counter and headed down the hall. I stood in my kitchen looking at the tiny whale carving in my hand. What secrets did it hold? Why had Aunt Rita kept it hidden away for all those years? And what should I do with it now? Mr. Chu had once told me the carving was valuable, but even with money tight, I'd never considered selling it. I was curious about whether there might be something inside it. I held it up to my ear and gave it a little shake. Did I hear something rattle inside, or was that just my over-active imagination?

I ran my fingernail around the line Dr. Brown had pointed out. There definitely was a seam there. I gave the tail a gentle twist. It didn't budge. I turned on the hot water faucet at the kitchen sink, and ran water over the carving, gently applying pressure to the tail until it moved a little. Slowly, I twisted the tail back and forth, until it started to turn more freely. I pulled it out of the water and dried it off on a dish towel.

I gently pulled on the tail. Like a stopper on a bottle, the tail released with a little pop. I looked inside the opening, then tipped the end into my hand. A tiny key fell into my palm. It was tarnished and old, like a miniature skeleton key. I had no idea what this might fit—I'd never seen any locked cupboards or chests among my great-aunt's belongings.

"Whatcha got there?" Val said, nearly scaring me to death. Val must've let herself in, and I had been so focused on my treasure I hadn't heard her sneak up on me.

"Geez, Val, you nearly gave me a heart attack!" Gumdrop hadn't made a sound—so much for my guard cat.

"Sorry. I wanted to see if that hunky vet had anything to say about me."

"As a matter of fact, he did. I think he'd like to get to know you better."

"Oh, goodie!" she said. "You still haven't explained what that little key is for." Val peered into my palm.

"I don't know. I just found it inside this little carving." I turned the key over in my hand, looking for any marking that might give me a clue to what this key fit.

"It might open a treasure chest!" Val said with an excited hop.

"Maybe, but we don't have a map to go along with it, so, it's going to be hard to know where to start digging."

"Oh, poo. And you haven't found any mysterious-looking chests?"

"No, but if I do, you'll be the first to know." I ushered her to the door. "Look, I'm tired. I'm going to call it a day. Oh, and Val? Here's Buff Brown's business card."

"Okay, thanks. I guess next time I need to take Stanley to the vet, I'll give him a call."

"He needs someone to paint his house."

"Sorry, I'm a little too busy to do that. Besides, Rudy would...oh, do you think I should call Buff and give him Rudy's number?"

"Yes, I do!" I adored Val, but sometimes she wasn't too swift on the uptake.

"You sneaky little devil," Val said, giving me an air kiss and sashaying out the door.

I picked up the whale carving, put the key back into it, and slid the tail back into its end. Then I took it back to my studio and put it on the windowsill which held many of my treasures.

FIFTEEN

AT TEN FORTY-FIVE that night I drove to the Chanticleer Theater. I wore all black because that seemed like the best attire for creeping around a theater. When I arrived, I parked at the far end of the parking lot and watched as the actors and crew members from *Hamlet* left the building. Finally, Ryan stuck his head out the backstage door and spotted me. He waved. It was time.

I trotted to him and slipped inside, pulling a flashlight from my handbag.

"You be careful," he said, with a sexy smoothness in his voice that was hard to resist, especially in the dark.

"You're sure you don't want to accompany me?" I asked, starting to wonder if I should do this alone.

"Look, my days of getting in trouble are over. I've already lost my dream job helping you." And it was true. Ryan had gotten into a lot of trouble springing me from jail.

"I didn't ask you to break the rules," I said, after taking some deep breaths to steel my nerves for what I was about to do.

"I know, that's on me. Look. I'll stand guard, and if I see someone coming, I'll text you. Make sure your phone is on vibrate."

I flicked the switch on my phone and stuffed it in my pocket.

I'd left my jacket with the microphone on it at my house. I didn't want Zachary listening in on this, because he would definitely not approve.

Off I went into the dark backstage. As I passed through the wings, I saw my old lamp, now in place as the new ghost light, illuminating the stage. I scanned the theater's seating area with my flashlight as I went. I knew having a flashlight on would be a dead giveaway if there was someone else in the theater, but there was no way I could sneak around in the pitch black. I thought about turning on the lights, but I didn't have a clue where to find the switches.

I took the small flight of stairs that connected the backstage to the seating area, staying close to the wall as I went. I crept into the lobby and tried the box office door. It was locked. So far my snooping wasn't panning out. Windows, which looked out on Yesler Square, ran the length of the lobby, and while it was dark, anyone walking by could have seen me. I definitely looked like I was guilty of something, standing there in the dark with my flashlight on. Not wanting to draw attention from any passersby, I headed back into the window-free seating area.

The door to the rehearsal space in the Underground was open. I decided to take a look around downstairs, even though this was my least favorite place. I walked silently down the stairs and into the rehearsal space, panning the flashlight from side to side as I went. The room was as we had left it, with a circle of chairs around the perimeter. At the far end of the room was the hall where Tessa and I had been nearly trampled by five stampeding teen girls running from a rat. Now it was my turn to explore, and I hoped I wouldn't run into anything, or anyone, that would freak me out.

I stepped cautiously into the hall, keeping the flashlight's beam pointed ahead as I walked. It was cold and creepy in this narrow passage—more like an underground alley, its brick walls lined with junk. There was a box marked with the word *Pyro*, as well as discarded props and set materials. As I continued along, the hall forked. Which way should I go? My sense of direction was abysmal, and even worse in the dark and underground. With a mental coin toss, I veered right, hoping this direction might take me somewhere useful.

After just a few yards, I came to a stairway that led up to a door. Pushing the door open, I found myself, amazingly, inside the box office.

I'd been in here before, when I talked with Daniel while he was working on his laptop. The ticket service window was closed up tight, so I decided it was safe to turn on the lights. I flipped the switch on, blinking against the sudden brightness. I was disappointed to discover that the laptop was nowhere to be found. Daniel must take it home with him at night. Dammit. I started looking for financial records that could help Bev. I opened the file cabinet, hoping to find a treasure trove of documents. There were documents, but none that would help us in the slightest. The whole top drawer was full of scripts. Double dammit. I tried the bottom drawer. It was full of actors' headshots. Triple dammit. The one sitting right on top was Ryan's, featuring his signature smoldering smile that made me weak in the knees.

I didn't want to return from my snooping mission empty-handed, but there was simply nothing in this office that could prove the Greers were laundering money. There were no clues about any drugs that might have been part of the reason Austin had been killed. I'd reached a dead end, for now, and it was time to get out of here.

I slipped back downstairs, and found myself at the fork in the alley. I was pretty sure if I turned to the left at this point, I'd find my way back to the rehearsal space. I crossed my fingers and made the turn. Moments later I was relieved to be back in the safety of the rehearsal space. I let out a deep breath. While I knew it was impossible to have held my breath the entire time I was in the passageway, it certainly felt like that. I was feeling a bit lightheaded, but that might have been more residual fear than a lack of oxygen. I steadied myself on a chair and listened. Above me, I swore I heard the sound of footsteps. Was someone here in the theater with me? I hoped not.

I realized—too late—that this was a bad plan. I needed to get the hell out of here. I was in a place where someone had been murdered only days before, and being here now had put me in danger with no backup plan. Had I worn my mic, I could have at least yelled my mayday word, ice cream. Great. Now I was scared and I wanted a bowl of ice cream.

I listened again for the sound, but heard nothing. It was time to make a break for it. I tiptoed up the stairs and into the backstage area. As I was passing through the wings, I glanced onto the stage. It was completely dark. What had happened to the ghost light? It had illuminated the stage and the audience area when I first arrived and walked through the seating area to the lobby. Now, the light was out. Had the bulb burnt out, or had the someone I'd heard walking around up here turned it off?

I stopped in my tracks. I had to find out. I crept onto the stage. Maybe this was all in my imagination. Maybe there was no one here. Maybe the light bulb had burnt out, though I clearly recalled watching Daniel install a new bulb. I walked to the center of the stage and flipped the switch on the ghost light. Light flooded the stage. Oh, no! Someone was in here with me. My stomach churned with fear. I needed to get out, and fast.

Something caught my eye in the darkened window at the back of the theater—the booth where the technicians ran the lights and sound. I swore I saw some movement up there. My flashlight's beam wasn't strong enough to reach that far as I squinted into the darkness. Suddenly, the stage lights burst on, blinding me, as I looked into the auditorium.

This couldn't possibly be an accident or a malfunction. Someone was in the booth, and they were doing their best to scare me. I must admit, they were doing a damn fine job. Suddenly, the ghost of Hamlet's father appeared, his gauzy form eerily gliding in from the wings, headed straight for me. This was the last straw. There was no way I could stay in the theater a second longer. I bolted out the door, where I found Ryan sitting in his car. I slid into the passenger seat next to him, out of breath.

"Holy crap, Jax, you look like you've seen a ghost!"

"I did see a ghost. I'm pretty sure it was just the special effects, but it means someone's in there running the effects from the booth. I thought I saw someone up there for a moment, but I wasn't sure, until the ghost came after me. Do lights and special effects ever come on automatically?"

"Not that I know of. Here, let me hold you," Ryan said, reaching out for me.

"Um, no. That would be unwise." I needed to get out of there for a variety of reasons, including Ryan wanting to wrap his strong arms around me. Plus, someone was trying to scare me off, and succeeding. My cover was blown, I realized. Whoever it was now knew I'd been in the theater snooping around.

SIXTEEN

THE NEXT MORNING Dylan was sitting at my kitchen table. I'd called him the day before and invited him to come over early for breakfast before starting work in my attic. Val had said she wanted to try out a new recipe for French toast. It was always terrific to have someone like Dylan around to eat Val's food, because he was perpetually hungry. Even if Val's newest concoction was a miss instead of hit, Dylan would likely eat it.

Rudy arrived a few minutes later and pulled up a kitchen chair next to Dylan.

"Hey. Nice to see you, man," Dylan said, fist bumping Rudy. "Jax said I might be able to help you out."

"Have you ever put up drywall? How about painting, ever done any?" Rudy asked.

"Yeah, I've done some drywall and a little painting. I can do some electrical work—not licensed or anything," Dylan replied. "I'd be happy to help you. My schedule's really flexible—I just need to check some dates with Tessa."

"Sure, I'll give you a try," Rudy said. "If it works out, I might have some other jobs for you. Summer's always a busy season for me."

"I won't let you down," Dylan said. As we passed around the

plates of food, I noticed Val helped herself to several pieces of French toast.

"I thought you were on Sleeping Beauty's Diet. Does she allow you to eat French toast?"

"Oh, that was a dumb diet! You know how they get you to lose weight?"

"By eating fewer calories than your body burns?" I suggested. It seemed like a logical guess to me.

"Perhaps, but what they wanted me to do was sleep. Like all the time, I mean, literally stay in bed and sleep."

"Sounds fantastic to me," I replied. I never wanted to get out of bed in the morning.

"Not me! I've got to get moving every day. If I don't, I get all down in the dumps. I had to move on to the next diet."

"And what's that?" I asked.

"The Weekday Diet," she said.

"And that is…" I prompted.

"I can only eat things that begin with the letter of the day of the week. So, it's Friday, and I can eat French toast," Val said.

"Oh, lucky you. Looks like French fries, fajitas, and figs are also on your menu," I said, counting items on my fingers.

"I'm not sure what I'm going to eat when I get to Saturday and Sunday."

"Steak and sausages?"

"I suppose…"

"Sangria and soup!" I suggested.

"Good job, Jax. Way to help me with my diet," Val said, digging into her breakfast.

"No syrup?" I asked.

"Not until tomorrow."

Rudy and Dylan didn't make a peep while we talked about diets. They must have already learned to steer clear of asking women about such a sensitive subject. It was treacherous territory.

I didn't think Val needed to be on a diet, but if it made her happy, I was okay with that. I doubted she'd lose much weight on this so-called diet, because I could think of plenty of calorie-filled foods for each day of the week.

Val was spot on with her new French toast recipe, along with eggs, fruit, and of course lots of coffee. After a to-die-for breakfast, I followed the men back to the attic to consult on the renovation project while Val bustled around in my kitchen cleaning up.

The men grabbed the ghostly sheet-covered chair I'd been unable to move by myself and carried it down the stairs, a cloud of dust following them. They took it all the way outside onto my back patio next to my wrought iron bistro table. I didn't want to keep it in the house a minute longer than necessary, given how filthy the chair was.

"You want me to vacuum up here?" Dylan asked Rudy.

"Nah, we'll do that last. How about you spend some time putting in the insulation between the wall studs, so we can get ready for drywall. I'll start bringing up the supplies," Rudy replied.

Rudy went up to the attic and took some measurements for the floor, which was going to be a bit of a challenge. While the existing floor was sturdy, there were a few missing planks. It would be impossible to match the new and the old flooring material. Instead, we decided to install new bamboo flooring that clicked together in panels. Rudy would close up the gaps in the floor so that the new floor could be installed properly.

"What can I do?" I asked.

"You can pick up the paint supplies. After Dylan gets the insulation in, we'll do the wiring, get the drywall up. Two days, maybe three, we should be able to paint up there." Rudy gave me a list of supplies and told me to pick a paint color, then he got to work.

Val had nearly finished cleaning up the kitchen by the time I returned.

"What do you have on your agenda today?" I asked.

"Oh, nothing until this afternoon. Then I'm working at the salon," she replied.

"Would you like to go a mission with me?"

"Oh, of course, darling. You know how I love a good mission," she said, as she put away the last of the silverware.

"I was hoping you could help me pick a paint color for the attic."

"Oh, poo. That's a boring mission. What else can we do?" Val asked.

"I do have another idea." I was worried I wouldn't be able to gather enough jewelry together for the auction, and I was running out of time. I'd been thinking about Frankie. Even though he was a pain in the butt, I still didn't have an emcee . I knew what I had to do.

"I've got a better mission for us. Let's go talk with Frankie Lawton and see if we can convince him to come back and be our emcee, and maybe donate some necklaces. If we can, let's also see if we can find out what he knew about Austin, maybe get some insights into who might have wanted him dead."

"Now that's what I call a mission," Val said as she whipped off her frilly apron. "I even know where his shop is, so I'll drive Firefly. Let me grab my purse." Val had named her car Firefly, for reasons I couldn't understand. I thought she just wanted to have a car that had a fun name like my Ladybug, but she insisted it had something to do with an old sci-fi TV series. I tried not to ask too many questions about Val's science fiction obsession, because once she started talking about it, it was hard to get her to stop.

She ran next door and was back minutes later, her gold lamé purse slung over her shoulder and a sparkly necklace in her hand.

"Here's that necklace I'm donating for the auction," Val said.

"Thanks," I said, taking it from her and adding it to the growing collection of jewelry on my worktable. "It's going to go for a high price. You sure you don't want to keep it?"

"No way. I'm happy to donate it."

Val's car was behind the house, so we left through my studio. She climbed into her car, and, as usual, removed her high heels and threw them in the back seat. I got in on the passenger's side, but left my shoes on.

Frankie had a design studio and gallery in one of the swankier parts of Seattle. As we drove toward his shop, I realized I hadn't thought much about what I'd say to him, but I knew I had to try to convince him to be our emcee. It would also be interesting to see what he knew about the Greers. I wondered what insights he might have about Austin's murder. He'd told Rosie Paredes to stay away from Austin and Amanda Greer. She'd been pretty upset when I'd visited her a few days ago. Apparently, Frankie thought the Greers were dangerous—how could that be? It was possible Frankie had seen something that had spooked him at the theater, or he might have witnessed the murder. For all I knew, Frankie could have been the one to murder Austin Greer, although he didn't seem to be the type.

As Val drove, I realized she was circling the same blocks over and over.

"I thought you knew where we were going," I said as I pulled out my phone to look up the address for Frankie's studio.

"I'm using The Force. It's an ancient Jedi mystical power," Val said. "It's strong with me, and it's telling me where to go." She waved her long red-lacquered fingernails in a mysterious way just above the steering wheel.

"There is no such thing as The Force," I said, punching the keys on my phone, searching for Frankie's address.

Val ignored me.

"I sense Frankie's studio is this way," she said, making a sharp left turn that flung my shoulder into the passenger door.

"Ouch! Be careful! Now my shoulder hurts," I said, rubbing it.

"And...we're here!" Val said triumphantly, pulling to the curb. The letters FL, for Frankie Lawton, loomed high above us in fancy script on a shiny silver sign. Miraculously, she had found his shop. I begrudgingly stuffed my phone back into my handbag. Whether Val had succeeded in finding our way using magical Star Wars powers, sheer dumb luck, or something in between, it really didn't matter. She'd gotten us here.

"I don't believe it," I said, getting out of the car and staring up at the sign.

"Never doubt the Force, my young Padawan." Val reached in the back seat and grabbed a pair of high-heeled sandals and put them on. I wasn't sure they were the same ones she tossed there earlier, since she had a stockpile of shoes in her back seat. She grabbed her purse and huffed toward the shop—clearly offended I'd doubted her mysterious Jedi powers.

Inside Frankie's studio, we found the man we were looking for. He looked decidedly unglamorous with his bifocals on, busily connecting little bits of silver chain together with a tiny pair of jewelry pliers. His gallery was elegant, with pale gray walls and a black high-gloss floor that made me worried I shouldn't be wearing shoes while walking on it. Part of me wanted to glide across it in stocking feet, but I didn't think Frankie would be amused. While Frankie was usually wearing something colorful and flamboyant, today he matched his gallery—black shirt and pale gray trousers.

"Hello, Frankie," I said, as I closed the door behind me. Val immediately started buzzing through the store looking for pretty things to buy. Frankie tipped his head back to get a look at me, and, realizing he couldn't see more than ten inches away with his bifocals on, pulled them off and squinted.

"Oh, no. I know why you're here," Frankie said with a frown. He must have known I was going to try to convince him to come back and work on the gala. "Did Tessa send you? Because I'm not coming back. It's not happening."

"No, Tessa didn't send me. I came on my own. But, listen, we need you, Frankie. We're really struggling," I said. I didn't know him that well, though I had done business with him last year. He always seemed just a little too far out of my league, so it was hard to connect to him in a personal way.

"Excuse me, but this necklace is just gorgeous," Val said, holding up a sparkly crystal necklace made of dozens of multicolored faceted gems. I was pretty sure this was Val's way of buttering up Frankie so she could get him to help us. She was a pro when it came to getting people to do what she wanted them to do without them having a clue she was pulling their strings. If Val did indeed have The Force, this is how she used it—to charm people. "I love it! Is it for sale?"

"Of course," Frankie said. "I'll give you a good price on it, because it's a prototype. But seriously, I know you're not here to buy jewelry. What do you really want?" he asked turning his attention back to me.

"To be quite frank, Frankie, Val is here to buy jewelry. Me? You guessed right. I'm here to see if you'll come back and be our emcee."

"Sorry, that's just not going to happen. When your pal Tessa initially got in touch with me, I was flattered, honestly. But the Greers..."

"What about the Greers? I talked to Rosie, and she said you thought they were dangerous. What is that supposed to mean? She's so upset she won't even donate a piece of jewelry for the auction."

"Look, you don't need to know. Okay? Just know there's more to the Greers than meets the eye. Although, I doubt I used the word *dangerous*. That may be what Rosie thinks I said, but I'd say it's more like complicated. And I don't need things to be complicated."

"You know Austin was murdered, right?"

"No! I knew he was dead, but I thought it was an accident—" Frankie sighed. "That's what I mean about complicated. Austin and Amanda always had an agenda—you just didn't always know what it was. I'm certainly not going to be the one who spills it all out in the open. I don't want to be near any scandals. It's damaging to my brand," Frankie said, spreading his arms expansively to show off the wares in his swanky retail gallery.

"Right. I understand. But can you at least tell me who would want to harm to Austin Greer?"

"I don't profess to know all the people Austin harmed in his life. He was born with a silver spoon in his mouth. He seemed to spend a lot of time giving his money away and doing silly frivolous things like trying to keep that silly theater afloat. Who'd want to kill him for doing that? I don't know."

"But, how about in other ways?"

"You might as well know, because you're going to find out if you investigate. Austin and I were business partners for a while. I'm not too proud of what we did, but you know, it was before I'd made it big. He bought me out, so I did okay. Austin thought he was doing all of these people a favor by selling his product. Me? I just thought it was a quick way to make a buck. At the time I was a little short on funds. Of course, in the end, he sold the company for a hefty profit, and he came out in even better shape. The guy really knew how to land on his feet."

"What kind of business?"

"Penis enlargement cream," Frankie said, without blinking.

"And that's why you think he's dangerous? That must have been some serious cream," I said.

"Austin was crazy. You know the only one who is crazier? His wife. And you know what the problem is with crazy? You can't trust crazy people. Now, ladies, I need to get back to work. Can I wrap that necklace up for you?" Frankie asked Val, who was trying on the necklace.

Something had upset Val. I wasn't sure if it was his mention of penis cream, or Frankie's uppity attitude, but I could tell she was unhappy by the tone of her voice, which had gone up an octave or two.

"You know, I think I'm going to ask my boyfriend for this for my birthday," Val said, setting the piece back down on its fancy Lucite display pedestal. This was her way of telling me she had no intention of buying this necklace—her birthday had been a couple weeks ago, she didn't have a boyfriend, and if she wanted something, she would just buy it—she didn't wait around for someone to buy it for her.

"Thanks, Frankie," I said, turning to go. "You know, if you think of something—anything—that you think would help us find Austin Greer's killer, will you get in touch with the police?"

"Of course, of course. I wouldn't want there to be some crazy person out there killing people," Frankie said, replacing his bifocals on his nose and returning to his work. "Oh, and I promise I'll talk to Rosie and tell her that donating a necklace to your fashion show isn't going to be dangerous. It probably won't even be complicated."

"Frankie? Can I at least ask you this one tiny favor?" I asked.

"Talking to Rosie isn't enough? Sure, what can I do for you?"

"Could we possibly get some of your jewelry back that you took from the fashion show? I'm having trouble rounding up enough replacements."

"Look, why don't you take that necklace your friend likes, that ought to go with something," Frankie said. "And please, don't thank me, it's the least I can do."

He had that right. It was the least he could do, the rat.

● ● ●

"So, Val, what do you think?" I asked as we got back in her car.

"Do you know where I can get that cream?" she asked, looking not the least embarrassed.

"What? Why?"

"Not for me, of course! Just for future reference." Val started the car and made an abrupt U-turn.

"Clearly I didn't think you were going to use it yourself. I'm not sure. I've, um, never needed it before," I said. "But what I really meant was—what do you think about Frankie?"

"Seems pretty slimy to me," Val said as she accelerated through a yellow light.

"Slimy? Why?"

"He just doesn't seem that honest, like he's hiding something. You know, it's like when Captain Kirk and Mr. Spock were talking in this one episode—"

"Val. Please, no more Star Wars references today."

"Sorry, darling, but that was Star Trek."

"Whatever. Look, Frankie told us about his, uh, cream. It didn't seem like he was hiding much of anything," I said.

"Take my word for it, that was just to distract us. I don't know, Jax. Something tells me he knows more than he's saying."

I wasn't sure what to think about Frankie. He didn't seem like someone who would be willing to climb up into a scaffold to drop a chandelier on someone. He seemed more likely to poison someone. Which made me wonder—if he had access to whatever drugs were in his questionable cream he once sold, might he also have helped Austin get the drugs he needed to feed his addiction?

SEVENTEEN

VAL DROPPED ME OFF at home and then headed to her salon.

We still didn't have an emcee, thanks to Frankie's unwillingness to rejoin our team. We'd already saved the gala from being shut down, but now we were risking having to cancel it because we didn't have a host. I wracked my brains for an idea—someone we knew who would have the charisma to make it all happen. Someone who had good stage presence. Then it hit me. One of the most magnetic people I knew was Ryan Shaw. He was in *Hamlet* at the Chanticleer Theater, so he definitely knew his way around the place and was comfortable in front of an audience. If anyone could convince him to help us, it would be me. I knew Zachary wasn't going to like it, but desperate times called for desperate measures.

I started some coffee and went back to my studio to check on Gumdrop, since he wasn't sleeping in his favorite paisley chair. I found him on my worktable, on the towel I had placed there a few days before. He'd rearranged the necklaces for the auction in his quest to get comfortable. I had five necklaces, now that I had Val's donation. I added Dylan's necklace to the pile along with Frankie's piece. I was getting close, but wasn't done yet.

"Come on, you big baby," I said, picking him up, lugging him out to the living room, and setting him on the sofa. I grabbed a cup of coffee, joined Gumdrop on the couch, and made the call.

"Hey, Ryan," I said when he answered.

"I hadn't expected to hear from you," Ryan said, sounding a little cautious. "Are you feeling a little less shaky after last night's escapade?"

"I'm trying not to think about it. I have a favor to ask. We need someone who can be an emcee for our event for the Homeless Advocacy Team at the Chanticleer Theater on Sunday," I said.

"Sorry, I've got a gig."

"Working for Val's Uncle Freddie?" I asked.

"Not right now. It's sort of a freelance thing while Freddie's in rehab," Ryan said.

"Rehab? Val said he was touring." This was sad news. I had no idea Uncle Freddie was having trouble, and I wondered why Val hadn't told me.

"I would know if he was touring, right? I'm his bodyguard. I'd be with him," Ryan said.

"Right. You would be. So, he's in rehab? Did he have a drug problem?" I felt strange digging for information, but since Val had been secretive about this, I needed to get my answers from somewhere.

"Last year he started having a lot of knee pain—those high platform boots aren't doing him any favors, other than making him taller, but he won't stop wearing them. He started taking some painkillers, and I guess he got hooked. He needs a knee replacement. You know he's no spring chicken, even though he acts like it. Doing all those concerts was sort of doing him in, and he was using too many painkillers. He realized he had a problem and checked himself in."

"Geez, I wish I had known he was struggling with addiction," I said. I wondered why Val hadn't told me, especially since she over-shared pretty much everything else in her life.

"I don't think he really wanted the news to get out."

That was understandable. To us, he was Uncle Freddie, but to the rest of the world, he was rock superstar Freddie "Boom Boom" Roberts, and I was certain the tabloids would have a field day reporting on his drug abuse problems.

After I finished my call with Ryan, my brother called me back.

"Sorry, I did what I could to get access to the medical records for Austin Greer, but I didn't find anything. I'm not entirely sure why—could be he didn't believe in seeing doctors, or it could be that I just couldn't get to the records because they've beefed up security on the servers at the hospitals. Or, he could have been getting his pain meds off the street. Sorry, sis, I think I've let you down."

"Thanks for trying. I really appreciate it."

"Hey, I'm happy to help you anytime." We said our goodbyes and hung up.

I wondered what insights Uncle Freddie might have into where Austin Greer had gotten his pain killers, given his own battle with addiction. I called Ryan back.

"Where is Uncle Freddie being treated?"

"Why do you want to know?" Ryan asked.

"Well, I wanted to talk with him about the drugs he was on. You see, one of things you don't know about Austin's murder is that he had a huge amount of narcotics in his system when he died."

"He did?" he asked, sounding as surprised as I'd felt when I found out.

"Yes, so much so he could have died from the drugs alone if the chandelier hadn't fallen on him."

"Wow, Jax, it sure does explain why he was acting so weird, flying off the handle at even the smallest thing, becoming nearly rabid if we didn't get everything just right when we were rehearsing. And then, after his tantrums, he would have moments of such calm we thought he'd fallen asleep."

"Wow is right. I only had one conversation with him, and he struck me as a bit of an odd bird, but I had no idea he was acting like that all the time. Actually, I did, because Tessa's daughters had told me as much, but I frankly didn't believe them. I do now. So, about that address where Uncle Freddie is staying…"

"You promise not to tell another soul?"

"Cross my heart," I said, fingers crossed he'd tell me.

"Château Glen View ."

"Thank you so much, Ryan. I owe you one!" I said goodbye and hung up, happy that Ryan always wanted to help me, regardless of the consequences. I hoped him spilling the beans wouldn't get him in trouble with Uncle Freddie.

I needed to find my way to the Château, and fast. I had some questions for Uncle Freddie. Since it was still early in the day, I decided I had time, since it was just a few miles out of town. It was a gorgeous May afternoon, so I put the top down on the Ladybug to enjoy the rare Seattle sunshine while I could.

As I pulled up to the facility, I didn't expect to be confronted with a gate and a guard. Honestly, I hadn't known what to expect, but I certainly hadn't thought it would be a high-security situation. It did make me wonder if all the gates and fences were to keep people out or to keep people in.

I drove up to the guard booth and said hello to a man wearing an official-looking black polo with a castle-shaped logo over his heart. I figured if I nonchalantly asked to come in, maybe he'd let me pass. No such luck.

"Hi, I'm Jax O'Connell, here to see Freddie Roberts."

The guard consulted his clipboard. Then he paged through a binder.

"Sorry, ma'am. You're not on the list."

"Dammit," I muttered. I didn't have a cell phone number for Freddie and I really didn't want to call Val and ask her for it. She might be upset I'd found out the truth.

"Is there any way you could call him and ask if he wants to see me?"

"Lady, you know how many people try to get in that way? Dozens. And you know what? It never works, so why don't you just take off. Don't embarrass yourself."

"Can't you just try?"

"Who are you—ex-wife, ex-girlfriend, ex-fiancée, ex-mistress?"

"No, I'm just the neighbor of his niece Val," I said, shaking my head, knowing my chances of getting in and seeing Freddie were less than zero.

"Val? Oh, hey, I know her. She gave me some advice on what to wear to my daughter's wedding. Hold on a second."

I waited while the guard turned his back and spoke into a walkie-talkie, before finally turning and pushing the button on the gate.

"There you go, ma'am. Have a nice day. He's in suite 74A. And say hi to Val next time you see her," the guard said.

"Will do, and thank you," I said, heading through the gates. I was starting to think Val truly did have some magical powers—just mentioning her name had gotten me into the Château.

As I snaked through the parking lot looking for the entrance that would take me to suite 74A, I thought about what the guard had said about Val. She had obviously visited her uncle here, because the security guard knew who she was. It saddened me to think Val had been too ashamed to tell me her uncle was in rehab. I'd have to decide whether I would even mention to her that I had been here to see her Uncle Freddie.

I found suite 74A and knocked on the door. Expecting some sort of nurse or attendant to answer the door, I was surprised when Uncle Freddie himself was standing before me. He looked less like a rock star than I had ever seen him, wearing sandals and a sweat suit.

"Jax! What a pleasure to see you," he said, pulling me inside his nicely appointed, but sterile, living room and giving me a hearty hug. "What brings you here? How'd you find me?"

"Ryan isn't always the best at keeping secrets," I said.

Uncle Freddie chuckled. "Yeah, he's a good guy, but he doesn't always have the best judgment."

I could agree with him on that, although I had benefited on more than one occasion from his poor decision-making skills.

"I came to ask you a favor," I said, getting right to the point.

"I'll always say yes to a friend of my little Valerie," Uncle Freddie said, escorting me to the sofa. As we walked together I realized how incredibly short he was—without his tall boots, he wasn't much taller than I was. Val must've gotten her height from the other side of the family.

"I'm sorry you're here. Are you okay?" I said, sitting down next to him.

"Me? Oh, I'm fine. I just found myself just a little too reliant on some little white pills. Far too many rock stars take far too many pills, and I didn't want to be one of them. Really, it's just a precaution being here. I don't want to end up like some of the more famous rock stars—dead."

"I'm glad to hear that, because I wouldn't want you to be sick or have an addiction or something," I said.

"You caught me on the best day, because I'm actually checking myself out of here."

"You can do that?"

"Of course I can. I checked myself in. I'm checking myself out. I think I better change, though, because if anyone sees me wearing a tracksuit they're going to wonder what happened to me."

"Can I ask you about the drugs you were on—I hope it's not too personal. I'm asking because someone died recently and he had high levels of opioids in his bloodstream when he passed away. He was murdered, so it's sort of complicated."

"Did he overdose? I've lost a lot of friends that way. That's why I was being extra careful, myself. Drugs—is that what killed him?"

"No, actually, it's pretty gruesome. A chandelier fell on him," I said, wincing at the thought of it.

"What a terrible way to go," Uncle Freddie said, shaking his head. "But I'm not sure how I can help."

"You got your drugs from a doctor, right?"

"Right."

"The man who died—his name was Austin Greer—we don't really know where he was getting his drugs. My brother, who's usually really good at finding things out like that, wasn't able to turn up any evidence that was the case. So, I'm pretty sure Austin was getting his drugs from someone on the street.

"You know, if you're addicted, you'll do just about anything to get what your body craves. So it's possible that if his doctor cut him off, he found another way to get what he needed," he said.

"Is that what happened to you?"

"I had doctors—stupid doctors—who were more than willing to prescribe me anything I wanted."

"I had this idea that maybe the person who killed Austin was his drug dealer, and something happened that made the dealer angry enough with Austin to want to kill him."

"See, here's the thing. He could've been hopping around from doctor to doctor getting his drugs, or he could've found an unscrupulous physician willing to prescribe the pills for him. You can't assume it was some sort of seedy drug dealer who killed that guy."

"Thanks. We'll have to keep looking. Freddie, you're a superstar," I said, giving him a hug.

"You got that right. And this superstar has to get out of here before they charge me for another day." Freddie grabbed his suitcase. "I'll walk you out."

"Can I ask you another favor?"

"Wow, two favors in one day—you're really pushing your luck," Freddie said, teasing me.

"Might you be available tomorrow night to be the Master of Ceremonies at a fashion show and auction? It's for a good cause. Even Val is helping us."

"Sure, sounds like fun. I cleared my calendar a few weeks back, so I can. Anything for you, Jax. You're like family."

• • •

Relieved I'd found an emcee for the gala, I called Jaya Bakshi at HAT to tell her the spectacular news while I sat in the Ladybug in the parking lot of Château Glen View.

"I'm sorry, Jax, but I'm afraid HAT is pulling the plug on the event. Without the chandelier, we aren't going to make much on the event. We've got to focus on restructuring our organization now that

Austin is no longer with us."

"'Restructuring?' What does that mean? You're not going to close down, are you?"

"My organization has had a difficult time working with Mr. Greer. We'd like to move on at this point."

"What do you mean 'difficult?'"

"He gave us a lot of money, but he was a real jerk about it. Always dangling money in front of me, making me beg him for it. It was disgusting. And the insults, the petty remarks, the sexual innuendo…"

"Oh, I'm so sorry. I had no idea."

"When he'd finally give us the money, I'd swear it was the last time we'd take anything from him. Now that he's gone, HAT is going to have to figure out how we'll go forward, if we can," she said.

"Couldn't you find other donors?"

"Yes, that's what we'll have to do. I regret it took Austin's death to realize I should have been looking for other donors long before now."

"That must've been hard, dealing with his insults."

"The board of directors kept telling me to suck it up. To take his money. There was no way to—"

"There was no way to get rid of him?"

"That's right. There was no way to get rid of him. Except kill him, and I can assure you, I'm not the one who did. But if I ever meet the person who did kill him, I'll probably shake their hand and thank them."

"Oh…"

"And if that makes you want to turn me into the police, that's fine. I've got nothing to hide. I can tell you this: I didn't kill him—"

"I didn't say you did. But at this point, I don't think you should be giving up on the event. We don't have the chandelier, but we have lots of other items. And isn't it better to make some money than no money?"

"I suppose," Jaya said with a sigh.

"And I did find a new emcee for the event."

"You did?"

"Yep. Freddie Roberts."

"*The* Freddie Roberts?"

"The one and only. He's a friend, and we're not going to have to pay him. So, what do you say? Can we do this? I know there will be a lot of people who will be glad if you say yes, including your board of directors."

"Okay, then, yes. And Jax? I do have an alibi for the night Mr. Greer died. If you are planning on siccing the police on me, you should know I couldn't have been the one to kill him."

"Of course," I said, hanging up the phone. I'd also make sure to tell Zachary every word Jaya had said, because anyone who had already thought through their alibi was certainly worth looking into.

My next stop was the local paint supply store. I picked up everything on the list Rudy gave me and selected a paint color— Lavender Mist, a pale purple that seemed soothing to me. It would be perfect for my newly renovated attic. As I waited for the clerk to mix the paint, I called Zachary and left him a message suggesting he check out Jaya Bakshi.

EIGHTEEN

NOW THAT THE GALA was definitely happening, I needed to find something beautiful to wear to the event. I knew I didn't want to have Val choose something for me, or else I'd end up in sequins and Spandex. I recalled the boutique I'd stopped at near the theater just a few days before, and since I was only a few blocks away, I decided a detour was in order.

I pulled to the curb in front of Styles by Cassie.

"Hello, and welcome back," Cassie said as I entered the shop. "Glad you made it back in. Are you ready to shop for something to wear to the gala?"

"I am."

I also had something else on my mind. She'd told me when we met she didn't have any jewelry because things hadn't worked out with her jewelry designer. Then I discovered Dylan was that designer. According to him, she said she was closing her store, which was why she'd returned his jewelry. I wanted to get to the bottom of it. It seemed to me that Cassie, who had made a snarky comment about the bad timing of Austin's death, was hiding something. If it had something to do with Austin's demise, I wanted to know about it.

"I'm looking for a little black dress," I said. "I've never really had one, and it seems like it would be a good basic piece for me to have. It would go with everything, especially my jewelry."

"That's right. You were going to bring me some samples of your work."

"Sorry, not today. This was sort of a spontaneous shopping trip. I promise I'll bring something by next week. But I do have a question for you. I'm friends with Dylan McCartney, and he seems to be under the impression that you're closing your shop."

"Oh, dear. Yes, that is a little difficult to explain," Cassie said as she fidgeted with the rings on her hands.

"Was there a reason you'd tell him that? Are you really closing your shop?" I asked as I started to browse the racks, hoping my nonchalant inquiry wouldn't make her defensive.

"More like wishful thinking."

"I don't understand. So you're not closing?"

"Not that it's any of your business, but I got an offer from a real estate developer. He wanted to buy my building, and all the rest of the property on the block, including the Chanticleer Theater. So, I got ready to shut things down and move to the Fremont District. That's why I told your friend I was closing up shop." I nodded and listened as I continued looking for the perfect dress. I'd gathered a couple of options but didn't want to stop while Cassie was willing to fill me in on what was going on. "Stupid Austin, he refused to sell. He said the theater was too important to him." She was getting a little red in the face. I could tell she was upset about what had happened.

"I guess he must have really loved that old theater," I said, thinking about why some people irrationally hold onto things at times.

"I can't explain the actions of that lunatic. He could have made a fortune selling the theater, and I could have made some serious money too, but only if we were both willing to sell.

"I guess he cared more about the theater than the money. I don't think he needed the income," I offered.

"Yeah, well, he sure liked to be a goody-two-shoes. It's too bad he couldn't have done some good in this neighborhood. This location is getting worse and worse. That's why I put those security gates up—too many break-ins in recent months. I was hoping they'd tear all this down and put up some nice condos."

"But with him gone, maybe his wife will want to sell the theater. That would be good, right?"

"From what I hear, the developer has moved on to a new project. He might reconsider building condos here, but I doubt I'll ever get that generous offer again," Cassie said, as she tidied a stack of scarves, trying her best to control her temper.

"I'm sorry. I'm glad your shop is still here because I think your clothes are wonderful." By now I'd collected three dresses to try on and was hoping one of them might be perfect for me to wear to the gala. Slipping into the changing room, I tried on the dresses. The first two didn't work for me, but the third one fit perfectly. I exited the dressing room, twirled in front of the trio of mirrors in the corner of the shop, and admired the dress.

Cassie stood behind me and nodded her approval.

"It's perfect. I'll take it," I said.

I wasn't sure what to make of Cassie's situation, but it did put her on my list of potential culprits, especially since her last name started with MO. She might have been angry enough with Austin, having lost the opportunity to sell to the developer, that she would want him dead. I couldn't be certain, but I wondered if she might have access to the theater via the Underground. I'd only explored one of the passageways under the theater, but if my somewhat faulty sense of direction was correct, the other subterranean alley led to Cassie's shop.

I paid for my purchase and walked the short distance to the theater. I was hoping I could catch up with Tessa, who seemed to be going at full-tilt to get ready for the gala.

Spotting the Starbucks where Tessa and I had taken Daniel the morning he discovered Austin's body, I popped over and picked up coffees for Tessa and me. Then I made my way to the theater, where I saw something that nearly made me drop both cups: Ryan Shaw, in cuffs, being hauled out of the backstage door by a uniformed police officer. Zachary emerged right behind them.

"What the hell! What's going on here?" I asked, rushing toward them. I was furious. Why hadn't Zachary told me Ryan was a suspect? I had dutifully been telling him everything about my progress, but he hadn't told much of anything.

"Arresting him for the murder of Austin Greer," Zachary said, in his sternest detective voice.

Zachary and Ryan had been jealous of each other since they first met, and Zachary had been at least partially responsible for Ryan losing his job at the police department. Now it had come to this. While I knew Ryan hadn't always played by the rules, I couldn't imagine he'd ever kill someone.

While the officer stuffed Ryan into the back of the police car, Zachary took me aside to talk privately.

"Look, I'm sorry. But it all adds up. He had an opportunity to kill Mr. Greer—he was at the theater the night of the murder. He had the means—according to Leslie Dreyfus, the stage manager, Ryan helped her hang the chandelier along with the artist. Since he knew how to hang it, he certainly knew how to tamper with it."

"But couldn't it mean that Leslie was the one who tampered with it? She could be pointing you toward him to deflect the blame away from her. Don't forget, she was at the theater with Ryan working the ghost special effects the night Mr. Greer was murdered," I said. I felt bad throwing Leslie under the bus, but not that bad, given how she'd treated us—including the Scottish play nonsense.

"I understand that. But she also told us he was alone in the theater well after rehearsal ended last night. We need to understand what he was doing in there, sneaking around, perhaps trying to cover his tracks."

This was not good news. Someone knew Ryan had let me in—but it couldn't have been whoever spotted me, because Leslie thought it was Ryan who had been inside the theater. I needed to make sure I didn't tip my cards because Zachary—if he didn't know already—would be unhappy to hear I'd been in the theater. I should have told him I was going before I went, but I knew he wouldn't have approved. And now, it felt too late to break the news to him. I had to proceed with caution.

"How does she know that?"

"Because the alarm system timestamps the security codes entered to arm and disarm the system. Rehearsal ended at eleven. Ryan didn't enter his code to lock the building until midnight. We've yet to discover what he was doing here."

Dammit. I was going to have to confess. But confessing wasn't going to get Ryan released. Maybe there was another way.

"What about a motive?"

"Jax, look, I know we're trying to work together—"

"Trying? I thought we actually were working together."

"Yes, of course. We are working together. I've been doing this a long time. We wouldn't go and arrest a suspect unless we thought he was the killer. He had a motive."

"What is it?"

"I'm not at liberty to say."

"I thought we were working together—you know, sharing information?"

"Right, and so let me ask you this: What haven't you told me? I've been a detective a long time, and I've also gotten to know you pretty well."

Dammit. He was on to me. I must be leaking guilt. Zachary was going to be angry to hear this, but he needed to know—he already knew something was up.

"Um. I need to tell you something," I said. I took a deep breath and plunged in. "Ryan let me into the theater last night.

"What? Are you insane? You were creeping around the theater by yourself, days after there had been a murder?"

"Well, if you put it that way, it sounds pretty bad. But, I was just trying to help with the investigation. I hadn't been able to get into the box office to look for records during the day, so I thought I'd try at night."

"With no listening device," Zachary said.

"Right. I didn't want you to worry."

"You didn't want to me know. You didn't trust me."

"No, that's not true. I do trust you. I wanted to help."

"Right. Well, I'd rather you not end up in the fridge in the medical examiner's lab."

"Me too. I know it was reckless. I should have told you. I'm sorry. Ryan let me in, but he wasn't in the theater with me, and it wasn't his idea."

Zachary removed his glasses, which usually made me all squishy inside. He pinched the bridge of his nose, and slowly blinked once, and replaced his glasses. Then he gathered me up in his arms and hugged me tightly.

"I just don't want anything to happen to you," Zachary said, kissing me on the top of my head.

He relaxed his arms and released me. Without a word he turned and trotted to the patrol car. I watched in amazement as Zachary helped Ryan out of the back of the car and ordered an officer to unlock the handcuffs binding him.

Ryan was free. But for how long?

NINETEEN

I THANKED ZACHARY for letting Ryan go, then I scanned the parking lot, looking for Tessa's van, but it was nowhere to be found. With two cups of coffee still in my hands, I gave one to Zachary as a peace offering, then pointed the Ladybug toward the Fremont District. I had to complete one final mission for the day. I needed to see Rosie at Aztec Beads about a necklace for the auction. By now, Frankie should have gotten in touch with Rosie to tell her it was okay to donate something. I crossed my fingers that he'd done what he promised, because time was running out. Once I had her necklace, I'd be up to eight, and I was hoping Tessa could supply the last two.

I parked the Ladybug at the curb beside the bead shop. As I entered, Rosie bustled up to me.

"I know why you're here. Frankie called me," she said.

"Oh, good." I relaxed a little now that I knew I wasn't going to have another dismal interaction with her.

"Listen, Jax, I'm sorry I didn't help you before. It's just that Frankie can be such a drama queen. I didn't know what to do or whether I should believe him or not. But, I do have a necklace here for you. I hope it brings in a lot of money for HAT," Rosie said, reaching around the counter and grabbing something off a lower shelf behind her.

"Thanks, Rosie, I really appreciate it."

She pulled out an elaborate necklace from a velvet tray. It was a beautiful combination of beads in all the colors of the rainbow. In a word, it was a treasure.

"Now, this is a special piece. I'm only giving you this because, you know, Dylan was homeless for a while. I think he could've used something like HAT back then to help him."

"It's beautiful, Rosie. Really. Did you make it?"

"Actually, Tracy made it. Pretty good, I think." Tracy was Rosie's daughter and Dylan's girlfriend. Tracy's young son, Benny, often played at the bead shop, and today was no exception. He was running around in the yard behind the shop with their little dog Tito, which I was thankful for. It meant Tito wouldn't be trying to attack me while I talked with Rosie. "She took all the random beads she found on the shop floor over the years and squirreled them away. Then she made them into this woven necklace."

"It's truly a work of art. Thanks so much. I'm sure it will fetch a good price at the auction, and I'll make sure we find the right person to wear it in the fashion show. Do you want to come to the gala? I can get you a free ticket."

"Oh, no, not me. I'm babysitting Benny tomorrow night so Dylan and Tracy can go out," Rosie said as she carefully wrapped the necklace in tissue paper and placed it in a box. "I hope it's a success."

It was dark by the time I got home and rolled into my parking spot behind the house. As I got out of my car, I was alarmed to see the back door standing open. Since Gumdrop was an indoor kitty, I was careful never to leave the door open. If Val had come over, I'm sure she wouldn't have left the door open, either. Dylan and Rudy had been working in the attic, but I didn't think either of them would forget to lock up when they left.

Being careful to not make a sound, I quietly opened the car door and didn't close it. My heart was pounding as I crept to my studio and peered through the window. The lights were off, and I could see someone moving through the darkness.

A burglar!

I stood, frozen, not knowing what to do. I often joked that Gumdrop was my guard cat, but in reality, he had never done anything to keep me safe. I wished Val's dog was visiting, because he might have been able to scare off whoever this was.

I crouched low behind the sheet-covered chair Rudy and Dylan had moved out of the attic. The thief crept out the door, a black hoodie pulled tight over his head. I caught a glimpse of what looked like a Venetian mask covering his face.

Suddenly, an orange kitten leaped from the roof and landed on the thief's head. The kitten's claws dug deep into the hood as the thief grunted and swatted at it. Then the kitten jumped to the ground, scurrying off into the bushes beside me. I stayed completely still, worried the intruder might spot me, while the sound of my pulse rattled in my ears. Without a sound, the burglar ran between my house and Mr. Chu's and disappeared into the darkness.

Frozen with fright and too shaky to stand, I sat quietly, contemplating my next move. I didn't think the thief would come back, but I wasn't ready to leave my hiding place. I heard a small squeak and turned as the heroic kitten emerged from the bushes.

"Hello, little one," I said in a whisper. I wondered if she belonged to Mr. Chu, since he had cornered the market on cats in our neighborhood. I reached out to touch her. She turned and bolted, heading back into the bushes behind my house.

I headed cautiously inside, locking the deadbolt on the back door behind me. I never used the deadbolt, but I expected I'd be using it much more in the future. It looked like the doorknob was busted and would have to be replaced. I turned on every light in the house. Oddly—and fortunately—the house hadn't been ransacked. Nothing seemed to be missing. Whoever it was had left empty-handed.

I found Gummie hiding under my bed.

"Oh, no! Gummie. Are you okay?" I asked my cat, pulling him up and placing him on my bed. He seemed unharmed, but still a little under the weather from his virus. I was freaked out and I didn't want to be alone. While I knew I should probably call Zachary and tell him what had happened, what I needed most was someone a little more upbeat. Someone like Val. I went next door and knocked. Val opened her door and ushered me inside.

"What is it, sweet cheeks? You don't look so hot."

"Holy crap, Val, there was a burglar in my house!"

"No!"

"Yes, and as he was leaving, a little kitten scared him off."

"Two questions. Have you called the police? You said 'he'—how do you know it was a man? How did a burglar get scared off by a kitten? You don't mean Gumdrop, do you?"

"That's four questions. You're right, I don't know if it was a man, it could've been a woman. Whoever it was, they weren't much taller than me. I didn't get a good look at him, but he was wearing some sort of a mask and a hood. And, no, it wasn't Gumdrop. It was a kitten who jumped from the roof and onto the head of the burglar."

"Good kitty! And where is this hero now?"

"She ran off. I don't know where."

"Oh, poo. Well, I'm glad you're safe. Is Gumdrop okay? And how is your house?"

"Everything is fine. Whoever was in my house didn't take anything, as far as I can tell. I should call the police. I'm not sure if this is related to the murder at the Chanticleer Theater, but I better let Zachary know, too."

I noticed Val was wearing rubber gloves, a rubber apron, and little rubber booties. "Is this your newest sci-fi costume?" Val loved to go to science fiction festivals in full costume. Her most recent Princess Leia costume had been a hit at the Burien UFO Festival a couple of weeks ago. It was the costume Val said was the reason for her recent dieting obsession. The white form-fitting gown had looked great on her when I had seen it, so I had to wonder if this was the real reason she had decided to drop a few pounds. This particular costume, I couldn't figure out. "Something from Rocky Horror Picture Show, perhaps?"

"No, silly, I'm washing the dog. I took Stanley out for a stroll-n-poop earlier, and he found a dead bird and rolled in it. It was disgusting!"

A loud *ah-roo* echoed from Val's bathroom. Stanley must have been distressed that Val had left him alone, and she headed down the hall to find him.

"Can I borrow your phone?" I asked. I'd left mine at home when I came dashing over to Val's.

"Sure, sweet cheeks, it's on the kitchen table."

I sat down at the table, picked up Val's rhinestone-encrusted phone, and dialed Zachary. Fortunately, I knew Zachary's number.

"Grant," he said, picking up the line. He always sounded so serious when he answered the phone when he didn't realize it was me calling.

"It's Jax."

"Oh, I didn't recognize the number." His voice softened and just hearing it helped to calm me.

"I'm using Val's phone. I, um…" My words caught in my throat. The fact I'd interrupted a burglar, and the danger associated with it, swept over me now that I was talking with Zachary. "Someone broke into my house." My voice cracked a little as I held back tears.

"Are you okay?" Zachary asked.

"Yes, I just kind of caught the guy as he was leaving, I think."

"Where are you now? Are you safe? Do you want me to come over?"

"I'm at Val's. You don't need to come, I'm okay. Sorry I called so late."

"Don't be sorry. You can call me anytime. Are you sure do don't want me to come over?"

"No, you don't have to. I'm really okay, just a little spooked."

"I think you should go away for a little while—I think perhaps your involvement in this investigation may have put you in danger," Zachary said.

"No, I'm fine. We don't even know if this break-in was because of the Greers. It could just be a random event."

"Maybe you could visit your parents in Florida?"

"Really, I'm okay, and I'm not running away to Florida just

because someone breaks into my house. I don't even think whoever it was took anything."

"Do you know what they could be after?"

"No idea. Should I call the police about the break-in?"

"Let me give dispatch a call. I'll have them send an officer over. I'll let them know you're at your neighbor's so you don't have to wait around the house by yourself. You're sure you don't want me to come over and keep you company?"

"Positive," I said. We said our goodbyes, and I hung up Val's phone, returning it to where I found it.

I followed the splashing sounds emanating from the bathroom, where I found Stanley chest-deep in a tub of sudsy water. As soon as he saw me, he started wagging his fat tail, which sent a tidal wave of water out of the tub and onto the floor.

"Now you can see why I need this kind of coverage." Val knelt at the side of the tub and started rinsing the dog.

"Listen, I need to tell you something."

She stopped rinsing. "What's wrong, honey bunny?"

"It's about your Uncle Freddie. I know where he is. Or, where he used to be."

"Oh—you know about the painkillers and the rehab? I'm sorry I fibbed about him. I wanted to tell you, but I needed to make sure it was okay with him first. I'm sorry I didn't tell you the truth."

"It's okay. It really is. I saw him today and he was doing really well. Actually, he's on his way home. He checked himself out. But I wanted you to know that I knew, because he's going to be our emcee at the gala tomorrow!"

"He is? That's fantastic! I love that. He'll be super, much better than that awful Frankie guy, anyway."

"I couldn't agree more. He's is going to be fantastic."

I saw two clear plastic bags of cotton balls on the bathroom counter. "Stocking up on cotton balls?" I asked.

"Yes—they're for my newest diet. You know, I had to give up on the Weekday Diet—there were just too many things to eat on Friday alone—French dip sandwich, fruit, feta, falafel. I ate all those things.

I'm still stuffed!"

"So what's the diet? Wait, don't tell me. You're not seriously going to eat them, are you?"

"They're supposed to be very filling and zero calories. I guess they help you feel full so you eat less. It seemed like a good idea."

"No Val, it's a very, very bad idea. Cotton balls can get caught in your digestive tract and cause a blockage—you could end up in the hospital, or worse."

"That would be terrible. Who'd take care of you, Gumdrop, and Stanley?" Val asked. I could take care of myself and the animals, but that wasn't the point.

"Why all the crazy diets, anyway? I mean, you've never been on a diet before, and you don't look like you need to lose weight." Val was naturally curvaceous, but nothing about her told me she was overweight. Even if she was extra voluptuous, she always seemed to love her looks and wanted to flaunt all she'd been endowed with and then some.

She pulled the wet dog out of the tub and toweled him off.

"I haven't had a boyfriend in a while and I thought...well...I thought...maybe there was something wrong with me," Val started to choke up. She stopped drying Stanley and used the edge of the towel to dab the corner of her eyes. Stanley took that opportunity to shake the rest of the water off, which doused us both from head to toe.

"Ugh! Stanley!" I grabbed a towel from the rack and dried myself off. As Val busied herself with the dog, I snatched the bags of cotton balls and made a break for it. "There's nothing wrong with you, Val, and I think Buff Brown would agree with me that you're perfect."

As I entered Val's living room, there was a knock at the front door. This was likely the police officer I was waiting for. I looked through the door's peephole, but it wasn't a uniformed officer. It was Zachary, and he had not one, but two pints of Molly Moon's ice cream.

I let myself out of Val's house, taking her latest problematic diet accoutrements with me.

"What are you doing here?" I asked as I took one of the pints from him. "Ooooh, salted caramel."

"What kind of boyfriend would I be if I didn't come over and see you after someone broke into your house?"

"I don't know, maybe the kind who listens to what his girlfriend says? I said I didn't need you to come."

"But I wanted to come." He wrapped his arms around me in a huge hug.

Val must have heard us on the porch, because she opened her door and found us there in a tight embrace.

"Oh! Well, I didn't want to interrupt, but um, maybe you two want to take whatever is going on there inside. This is a family neighborhood," she said with a giggle, and then shut her door.

We put the ice cream in the freezer for the time being, and then walked through the house together. I confirmed that nothing been stolen.

"Do you want to file a report?" Zachary asked.

"Since nothing is missing, I don't think so, but do think I'm ready for some ice cream," I said, as I headed for the kitchen in search of my ice cream scoop and some bowls. I made us each ridiculously large bowls of ice cream—salted caramel and a flavor called melted chocolate—and we sat on my little patio eating it. It was the perfect end to a not-so-perfect day.

TWENTY

THE FOLLOWING MORNING I awoke to the sound of my phone ringing. It was Bev.

I answered, still groggy from a fitful night's sleep.

"I listened to your cat purr for far too long yesterday afternoon, and I'm getting awfully tired of it. I'm hoping you'll remember to wear your mic today."

"Sorry, Bev, I left the jacket with the mic on it on my bed. Sounds like my cat was sleeping on it. I won't let it happen again."

"Any news?" Bev asked.

"Yes! Last night when I got home I interrupted a burglar. It was scary, but it doesn't seem like they took anything."

"Oh, hon, I'm sorry to hear it. Did someone from the department stop by?"

"Yeah, actually, Zachary came by, and together we looked the place over. Nothing appears to be missing. Oh, but there is something you should know. I explored the theater the night before last and was able to get into the theater's box office, but I wasn't able to find anything important. The file cabinet was filled with scripts and headshots. Daniel must have taken his laptop home with him."

"Damn. I thought you'd be able to find something. The Greers must keep their records at their house. Any chance you're going to be able to make it over there sometime soon?"

"As a matter of fact, I want to go to the Greers' house this morning to buy some beads. I'm hoping I'll be able to do some snooping while I'm there."

"Good job, Jax. I have faith in you."

"Thanks. I promise I'll report back."

"You can do better than that. Wear the damn mic."

I called Nika and told her I was ready to buy some Thai silver beads. As luck would have it, she was available to have me come over right then, as I had hoped. I jumped in the Ladybug and headed to the Greer mansion. I checked the mic in my little boutonnière on my jacket just before I headed up the long driveway. I followed it around to the right, as Nika had instructed, to arrive at the side entrance of the converted carriage house that served as the storage facility for Amanda's bead business.

"Knock, knock," I said, poking my head in the door of the bead warehouse.

"Hello, Jax. Come in," Nika said, handing me a basket. "Just fill up this basket with whatever you'd like to purchase. Mrs. Greer said you could have our wholesale discount."

I looked out across the dozen long wooden tables that held thousands of six-inch strands of silver beads in every shape and size imaginable, from small plain disks the size of sunflower seeds up to silver-dollar-sized pendants. I walked up and down the aisles between the tables, selecting a few strands as I went. Nika busied herself at the laptop on one side of the room, near another door that stood ajar. What I needed was for Nika to wander off and leave the computer unattended, but that seemed unlikely.

I decided to see if I could find a reason for Nika leave so I could do some snooping without her around.

I yawned. Then waited and hoped. There was no reaction from Nika. She just kept typing on her laptop. I yawned again, even louder than the last.

"Oh, dear, I'm so sorry. I've just not been getting enough sleep lately," I said, trying to be as obvious as possible. I hoped she'd be the polite hostess she'd been the last time I was here and ask me if I'd like coffee. Finally, she did.

"I could make coffee. Would you like that?" Nika asked, looking up from her laptop.

"If it wouldn't be too much trouble," I said as I tossed a few more strands of beads into my box.

"No trouble at all. I'll be right back," she said. I waited until she left, heading down the long breezeway that took her to the main house.

I sprinted to the laptop and carefully looked at the screen, filled with spreadsheets, an email program, a mailing list, and an order processing system. I should have brought a thumb drive with me so I could copy some of the files that looked like they might be useful in the investigation, but I hadn't thought of that, and now it was too late. I looked under Nika's desk and in the file drawer. Nothing was there except her stylish monogrammed purse stuffed in a drawer.

Next to the laptop, the storeroom door was ajar. This was the small storage space where Amanda had taken the necklace she'd given me for the auction. It contained two more tables full of silver necklaces. Perhaps they kept these in this room because they were more valuable. The price of silver had been on the rise and storing the more expensive pieces in this room might have been a security measure.

I moved across the room to another table of small beads, so I didn't look guilty of snooping when Nika returned. I was sure she'd be back soon, and I didn't want to be caught looking suspicious.

"I'm so sorry to take so long," Nika said, entering the warehouse, her voice echoing off the walls.

She poured coffee into a dainty china cup with a floral design and handed it to me.

"Thanks," I said, adding some cream and sugar to the cup and took a few sips of the coffee. It was delicious. "Such great service." I continued drinking my coffee and shopping, figuring I should buy as much as I could afford since I wouldn't get another opportunity to get such a steep discount, plus the longer I stayed, the more likely it was that Nika would leave me alone so I could do some more sleuthing. I knew I could use many of these beads in some of the earrings I made, so I tried to think creatively as I shopped. Unfortunately, I found I wasn't thinking very creatively. In fact, I was having trouble thinking at all.

And I was feeling tired. Wasn't coffee supposed to wake me up?

And then I was feeling a little woozy.

And a little lightheaded.

And then the darkness closed in around me.

When I woke up, Nika was crouching next to me. I was laying on the cold concrete floor beneath one of the tables.

"Jax? Are you awake?"

"I think so." Although I was having trouble keeping my eyes open.

"Then maybe you can tell me what this is?" Nika asked, holding something small and colorful a little too close for me to focus on it. I pulled back my head to get a better view.

"Oh, that's my boutonnière. Careful, there's a mic in it." Why in hell had I just said that?

Nika placed the boutonnière on the floor and crushed it with the heel of her shiny black pump.

"Why did you do that?" I said, trying to sit up. But, somehow, my body didn't want to do what I wanted it to do. "What's wrong with me? Oh my God! You drugged me!"

"Don't worry, it'll wear off, eventually. Now, Jax, we're going to make this easy. Okay?"

"Okay," I said, not knowing what I was agreeing too. Everything was feeling pretty easy right now, other than focusing, talking, or sitting up.

"Who are you working for?"

"Um. I work for myself. I'm a glass beadmaker, but you know that, Nika. Okay. Now I get to ask a question. Why does your purse have an M monogrammed on it?"

"Sorry, that's not how this game works. How it works is you tell me what I want to know, and you won't get this." She reached into her pocket and pulled out a syringe full of milky white fluid.

"Yeah, I don't want that," I said, groggily shaking my head.

"So, you're going to tell me who you are working for."

"My boy Zee," I said, barely coherent.

"Jax, you're not making much sense. Do you need a little shot?" Nika said, grabbing my arm. With all my might, I flipped my body over onto my side, yanking my arm away from her. Using every wobbly muscle I had, I wriggled away from her, like a giant fish out of water, flopping around on the shore.

"Why is there an M on your handbag?" I asked again, my addled brain was unwilling to let that go. It didn't make sense. And then it hit me. People called me Jax, because I didn't like Jacqueline. And Nika, what was it short for?

Monika.

"Monika," I whispered to myself, but I couldn't really tell how loud my voice was. It must have been louder than I realized.

"Congratulations, Jax. You figured it out. My name's Monika. Wow, you really are a super sleuth," Nika said, her voice thick with sarcasm. She crawled toward me under the table, with the syringe in her hand. I kept wriggling, staying just out of reach. "Now, what I really need to know is what else you know."

"I don't know anything. I swear. I just came to buy beads...Oh, and to see if you might be involved in the murder of Austin Greer." Somehow my brain had short-circuited. Things were coming out of my mouth that I didn't expect. "So, if you can just tell me what you had against him, I'll be on my way."

"Austin was just a stupid old man with all his do-gooder projects. Let's run a theater, let's work with a homeless agency, let's donate stuff to all the needy nonprofits."

"Yeah, he was so good, you had to kill him," I said.

"No, you've got it wrong. I didn't do it."

"But you know who did."

"No. I swear I don't."

"You're MO, that Austin wrote in his dying moments. He was trying to write Monika."

"It's not too hard to figure that one out, Jax, but he was wrong. I didn't do it."

"Why would he spend his dying moments trying to write your name?"

"He likely had figured out what Amanda and I were really importing. He wanted to point the finger at me, if nothing more than to keep the focus away from his wife."

"What are you importing?"

"Who would have suspected sweet Amanda Greer would be the biggest importer of heroin on the west coast? Certainly not you."

"But, she doesn't ever leave the house—she told me herself. How could she do it?"

"She used to make the trip a couple of times a year, but over time she became more and more afraid to go outside. That's when she asked me to take over. Poor thing, if she only knew that all the money coming in from her business has more to do with drugs than beads."

"You go to Thailand and bring back drugs?"

"See Jax, even in your drugged-up state, you're doing quite well figuring this all out."

"What did you give me in that coffee?"

"Oh, just a little intoxicating cocktail. Austin had a whole lot of it in his bloodstream when he died. Powerful stuff—it did wonders for him. I can't believe it didn't kill him. You seem to be handling it like a champ. I think you could use another dose." Nika crawled toward me, stopping to uncap the syringe with her teeth as she steadily moved underneath the table toward me. "Sadly, I didn't want to add murderer to my resume, but I think it's time for you to go. I can't have you telling the world what's going on here—it would ruin my path to Easy Street."

I used every ounce of strength I could muster and kicked my legs against the floor to get away from her. My foot came in contact with the wooden leg of the table, and I heard it crack. I kicked again. And again. Finally, the leg broke. The table crashed over, coming down on top of one of Nika's legs, pounds of silver beads pouring off the table on top of her.

"Oh God! My leg! You crushed my leg!" Nika screamed, trying to push the heavy wooden table and strands of silver beads off of her. "Help me, Jax. Please."

"Help will be here soon." I crawled to the end of the row of tables. Using hands that barely functioned, either from the drugs I'd accidentally consumed or from pure fear and adrenaline, I dialed Zachary. He picked up on the first ring.

"We heard everything up to the point when your mic went dead. We just arrived. Hold tight."

"Nika's going to need medical attention," I said, as I watched her writhe in pain. She found the syringe she'd tried to use on me and jabbed it into her thigh. She visibly relaxed. Within seconds, her eyes closed and her breathing slowed.

Zachary ran in the door of the warehouse.

"Are you okay?" he asked, kneeling beside me.

"A little limp and wobbly, but I'm okay. You should check Nika."

He ran to her side and checked for a pulse at her neck. He nodded his head. She was alive. Zachary called for medical support, and soon the EMTs were loading her into an ambulance.

"Make sure to keep a guard on her," Zachary said, as the medical technicians climbed into the ambulance with Nika.

"She—she—tried to kill me. She injected herself with something. Whatever it is, I'm not sure if she was trying to kill herself—"

"We're going to get you to the hospital, too. You're not looking so hot," Zachary said.

Things got a little blurry after that. Someone slipped an oxygen mask onto my face, and I felt a jolt of oxygen—that was good. And I felt the bumpy ride in the ambulance while someone held my hand. I opened my eyes, just a little, but the lights hurt. It was Zachary, sitting next to me, his glasses off and his eyes closed.

"My boy Zee," I said, though it was muffled through the oxygen mask.

"Shhhh," he said, kissing me on the forehead.

TWENTY-ONE

I WOKE UP IN THE HOSPITAL, still holding someone's hand. Expecting it would be Zachary, I gave it a squeeze, and realized it was far too small a hand to belong to him. It was Tessa.

"Hello, sleepyhead," Tessa said, seeing that I was awake. I pulled the oxygen mask from my face. "Are you sure you should do that?"

"I'm okay. I'm just glad to see you."

"*Dio Mio*, Jax, how are you feeling?"

"A little woozy."

Tessa reached over and hugged me. As I looked past her shoulder I discovered, to my surprise, the world's largest, and pinkest, teddy bear.

"Um, Tessa, who is that from?"

"Ryan. He came by and wanted to stay until you woke up, but I sent him away. I can't believe he'd buy you a stuffed animal, but I guess it is sort of cute," Tessa said, glancing over her shoulder at the hideous pink bear.

"That's sweet, but it's not really my style."

Poking out of the top of the garbage can by the door was a stack of used paper coffee cups. Clearly Tessa had spent many hours at my bedside.

"Any chance the hospital will let me have something to eat? Maybe some coffee?"

"Let me see if I can get a nurse," Tessa said, pressing the call button.

Moments later a young woman in floral scrubs bustled in.

"How may I help?" the nurse asked me.

"May I have something to eat?"

"Let's get a doctor in here to make sure that's okay." The nurse said as she checked my vital signs on the monitor next to my bed. "You stick around, okay? I'll be right back," she said as she rushed out the door.

A tall woman in a white lab coat entered my room and introduced herself as Dr. Phillips.

"How are you feeling?" she asked, much less hurried than the nurse had been.

"A little lightheaded, but that might be a lack of coffee," I said.

The doctor chuckled. "We have really rotten coffee here, so I suggest you get out of here and find something decent. I'll send the nurse to discharge you."

"Do you know what drug I took?" I asked the doctor.

"We're assuming an opioid, but what specifically, we don't know. We've been treating you with an anti-opioid medication called Naloxone, which stops the effects of narcotics. You've bounced back after a couple of doses, so I can only assume that is what you consumed. We're running some tests to verify, but we won't have the results for a couple of days."

"Am I going to be okay?"

"You should be fine. You might feel a little dizzy and lightheaded for day or two. I wouldn't go running any marathons if I were you."

"No chance of that," I replied, happy to hear I could get out of this place and return to leading my mostly normal life.

"If you're still feeling dizzy by the midweek, please get in touch with your doctor. If anything surprising shows up in your lab work, we'll be in touch," Dr. Phillips said from the doorway.

"Thanks," I said. Tessa helped me get dressed. The less time I spent in the hospital, the better. I asked Tessa how the fashion show and auction had been, as I suspected I'd been zonked out for so long I'd missed the event.

"You didn't miss it, silly. You're not like Rip Van Winkle. You haven't been asleep for years. The gala is tonight."

"Are you ready? Is everything ready? I mean, I didn't even—"

"Relax, everything is fine. We're ready."

"Do you think I can come?"

"The doctor didn't give you any restrictions, so as long as you behave yourself, I don't see why you can't go."

"But, did Val's Uncle Freddie get in touch with you? Does he know what to do?"

"We're ready. All you need to do is show up tonight. I'll make sure Zachary can bring you to the theater. You probably shouldn't drive quite yet."

The nurse arrived with several forms for me to sign, and I settled into the requisite wheelchair for the ride downstairs.

"I'm going to get the car," Tessa said, placing my handbag and the giant pink bear in my lap with a smirk and parted ways with us.

As I was wheeled down the corridor by the nurse, I noticed a uniformed police officer standing outside the open door of one of the patient rooms. Glancing into it, I saw Nika sitting on the side of the bed.

"Excuse me, can you please stop for a moment? I'd like to talk with someone." The nurse stopped. I got out of the wheelchair, grabbed the pink bear, and walked on shaky knees to the officer. "May I please visit the person in this room?"

"Sorry, ma'am, I've got strict orders not to let anyone in here," the officer replied.

"Oh, but I've got this adorable gift for her." I thought maybe a little guilt might help. "Please don't send me away without being able to give it to her."

"Ma'am, I've got strict orders. No visitors."

I wobbled back to the wheelchair, putting the bear in the seat, and grabbed my phone out of my purse. I made a call, and then took the phone to the officer.

"Yes, of course, Detective Grant." After a brief conversation the officer hung up and handed the phone back to me. It's good to have friends in high places, or a boyfriend who works in the homicide division of the Seattle PD.

"Go on in, but don't try and take her out of there," the officer said, chagrinned.

I entered the room and sat down next to Nika.

"I don't want to talk to you," she said, her arms folded across her chest.

"I just want to understand what you were doing. And why."

"Austin and Amanda—they had so much, but they didn't know how to use it. Austin spent all his time volunteering, trying to help the poor and the little people like me. Amanda—she spent all of her time trying to make more money so people would admire her."

"And the drugs—were you giving them to Austin?"

"He was in pain, and I was just trying to help. He'd fallen off the ladder at the theater and broken his hip, and he had a lot of pain for months and months. The doctor had been giving him Oxycontin but eventually cut him off. He said he didn't want Austin to become addicted. But it was too late. So, I did him a favor, I made some trades, and I got him the drugs he needed. I slipped them into his coffee. He was so happy to be pain-free—he thought he was finally well. I couldn't break the news to him that he was addicted to narcotics. Anytime I cut back, he'd get sick, and the longer he went, the angrier he'd get, until he was raging at everyone. I swear. I didn't want to harm him. I was just trying to help. Besides, if I told him, he would've wanted to know where the drugs came from. How was I supposed to tell him they came from his own wife's drug smuggling business?"

"But why did you care what happened to Austin?"

"Look, Austin decided I was his favorite little homeless girl. How could I resist that? He gave me a roof over my head and a job. The only thing I could do was ease his pain. How else could I ever repay him?"

"I don't know. Maybe by killing him?"

"That doesn't make sense, does it? I didn't want anything to change. Everything was going fine. Amanda was happy with all the money coming in, and that left Austin to run his theater and give it cash infusions whenever the coffers were empty. Me? I got a nice salary and some not-strictly-legal fringe benefits. If Austin were dead, then Amanda wouldn't need to raise money for the theater. She'd already told me she didn't want to keep importing. She was ready to retire, but couldn't stop as long as Austin continued donating everything she made, minus my cut."

"But why couldn't you just sell beads? You didn't have to smuggle drugs."

"Are you kidding me? You think I could make enough money selling beads to live a decent life?"

"I do. Mine aren't silver, they're glass, but sure, I make enough to make ends meet most months."

"We couldn't sell enough beads to fund Austin's little pet projects and donations all over the city. Such a philanthropist—if they only knew where the money was coming from."

"So, you're a drug trafficker, but not a murderer?"

"Something like that." She gave me a look that was hard to decipher—a mix of defiance and defeat.

The nurse with my wheelchair knocked on the door.

"Excuse me, but I think we should be going," she said, peeking her head inside the room.

"Wait. Just one more thing—how did you know I was working for someone to investigate you?"

"Come on, Jax. You're not a Tony Award winning actor." Nika gave me a disdainful sneer.

She rose on her crutches and headed for the wheelchair as if it was meant for her. The cop stopped her at the door.

"Excuse me," I said, barging past her, grabbing the pink bear, and plopping myself down into the wheelchair. "Let's go."

TWENTY-TWO

TESSA DROVE up the narrow alley between my house and Mr. Chu's and pulled in next to my car.

"Wow! How did the Ladybug get back here? I left her at the Greers," I said.

"Zachary took your keys and drove it back here. He's been worried sick about you, you know, but isn't too keen to sit idly by your hospital bed. He'd rather be out doing something. Oh, and he told me he put your purse and your keys on the kitchen table."

And for that, I appreciated Zachary more than he would ever know.

As Tessa helped me out of the van, Mr. Chu hurried across the alley with a small package in his weathered hands.

"Your friend, that man who brought your car back, he told me you were in the hospital. I have this little gift for you—from my shop."

"Oh, thank you, Mr. Chu," I said, accepting the package and attempting to hug him.

He waved me away. "You better get in bed, save your hugs for someone else." Mr. Chu, I had learned long ago, wasn't much of a hugger.

"I'll see you tonight at the auction. I've got to get ready and feed my cats. Otherwise, I won't be able to go," he said with a wave as he headed back across the alley.

Tessa settled me in bed with my package from Mr. Chu.

"You rest. I'll make sure Zachary picks you up and brings you to the gala. You just need to be dressed and ready by six. Okay? And you can call Val, she can help you, too. I've got to get over to the theater." Tessa gave me a hug and left. She was back a minute later with the large pink bear.

"You don't want to forget this," Tessa said, placing the bear on the bed next to me and dashing out the door before I could throw it at her.

Opening the small box from my neighbor, I discovered an egg-sized bronze sculpture of a chicken. How odd. I didn't have a particular affinity for chickens, but the sculpture was interesting and unusual. I would have to ask him about it when I saw him tonight. Testing out my wobbly legs, I slowly wandered back to my studio and placed it on the window ledge above my worktable among the many other treasures I'd collected over the years. After that, I rested on the sofa for a while, dozing on and off all afternoon. Gumdrop joined me mid-afternoon to knead his claws into my side.

"Geez, Gummie, why don't you settle down here with me?" My cat didn't say a word. He just walked back and forth across the couch. "Oh, I know, you want to be fed. I bet Val hasn't been feeding you."

Gumdrop and I padded across the living room to the kitchen. I was a still little lightheaded, but I felt like I was functioning pretty well given the circumstances. I scooped half a can of cat food into Gumdrop's bowl.

Val burst in my front door, startling both me and Gumdrop.

"Hello, my little honey bunches! How are you feeling? Tessa told me I should check on you. Are you okay? Do you need to—"

"Val, slow down, will you? I'm fine, just a little woozy."

"You can't go and get yourself killed, you know. Gumdrop needs you," Val said, crushing me in a hug.

"Just Gumdrop?" I squeaked as Val continued to squeeze me. "Um, Val? You can let go now."

"Oh, sorry. I need you too," she said, releasing me from her killer grip so I could breathe again.

"Whoa, Val—"

"Too much?"

"You're always too much and that's why I love you," I said, stabilizing myself by grabbing the edge of the kitchen table.

"I love you too and want to take care of you. It's also why I'm going to help you get ready for the gala."

"Oh, that's okay. I'm sure I can manage," I said. Val's high energy was taking its toll. I was already exhausted.

"No, I insist," Val said, charging toward my bedroom. "Let's see what we've got here." Val started flipping through the dresses hanging in my closet, muttering to herself as she evaluated each one, "no, no, no."

"Wait! I have a new dress," I said, rummaging through my handbag to find my car keys.

"Where is it?"

"In the trunk of the Ladybug." I tossed her my keychain.

Val popped out to the car and met me in my bedroom a moment later.

"Bravo! What a spectacular dress," she said, pulling off the plastic cover to get a good look at my little black dress. "I'm so proud of you. You picked this out yourself?"

"I did. And I even have some jewelry to wear with it. It's in the top drawer of my dresser."

Val found the necklace and held it up to the dress. The black beads with red polka dots and the red beads with black polka dots, strung into a short choker, worked perfectly. I was so happy I'd decided to keep this piece.

"That works for you. Me, I like something a little more sparkly." This was not at all surprising, because nothing was ever sparkly enough for Val.

"And speaking of jewelry, did Tessa get enough necklaces for all the outfits?"

"She did! We have ten, two for each girl. There are two from you, two from Tessa, one from Mr. Chu, one from me, one from Rosie, one from Dylan, one from Frankie, and one from Amanda Greer. It took some searching to find the silver one from Amanda—it had fallen down behind your worktable. Probably Gummie knocked it off."

"Sorry about that. Gumdrop has been spending a lot of time on that table rearranging things."

"Now, do you want me to help you with your clothes?" Val asked.

"No, I am capable of dressing myself. Besides, there are a couple of hours to go before the gala even starts. And, I think I need another nap."

I heard a double-honk coming from the street in front of the house.

"Oh! That must be Buff. He's taking me to the theater on his motorcycle. How exciting is that? The models will be arriving soon so I can do their hair and makeup. Take care, doll, see you tonight."

"Is that what you're wearing?" I asked her. She wasn't in one of her over-the-top outfits today. Instead, she was wearing all black.

"Everyone knows you must wear black when you're working backstage," Val said, as she posed like Vanna White so I could fully appreciate her skin-tight black leather pants and black long sleeve sweater with a plunging neckline. "See you tonight for the big event!" She blew an air kiss at me and headed out the door.

I followed Val to the door. I had to see this. She skipped down the front steps to Buff and his ride.

Buff handed her a leather jacket and a bright yellow helmet, which she pulled on with difficulty over her fluffy red hair. A fringe of bangs nearly covered her eyes, and a big puff of hair at the bottom edge of the helmet made her look like a demented lion with a shaggy mane.

"Do not laugh," Val shouted at me from the curb. She situated herself in the sidecar of the motorcycle, Buff gunned the bike's engine, and they were off. Val squealed as they drove away.

I didn't laugh—much.

Back inside, I wobbled back to my studio. I needed to find some earrings to match my necklace and dress, and having a little time to spare, I looked through my plastic storage bins for the perfect pair to pull from my inventory. I found some dangly seed bead earrings that were black and red—they'd be perfect with the rest of the outfit. It was good I'd found something I'd already completed. I wasn't sure if I could have managed to use my jewelry pliers to make new ones with wire and beads, since my strength wasn't back to normal quite yet.

Zachary arrived, as promised, at six. I had made it into my new black dress and matching jewelry. I'd even applied my standard makeup: bronzer and tinted lip balm. My lightheadedness had subsided into a low buzz at the base of my skull, which was a relief.

"You look fantastic. So beautiful," Zachary said, hugging me and giving me a gentle kiss on the cheek.

"It's my new dress, and see, I even had a necklace and earrings to match." I did a little twirl, which I realized right away was the wrong thing to do. I stopped and grabbed one of Zachary's arms. "Whoa! I guess I shouldn't do that."

"Are you sure you feel well enough to go?"

"I'm going. I just need to take it easy. No more spinning for me. Good thing I don't have to be on the runway tonight. I don't think I could make any of those high-fashion model moves."

"We'll leave that to Tessa's girls," Zachary said.

He looked handsome in his charcoal wool suit. Usually, his choice of neckties was terrible, but tonight, he'd picked something new—a bow tie.

"Oh, you look so cute in your bow tie," I said, pulling him close.

"I wasn't going for cute. I was going for respectable. I guess I missed the mark," Zachary replied.

"I like it. It's a keeper, and so are you." I found my handbag and checked my dress in the mirror by the door. "Any news on what drugs Nika gave me?"

"They're working on it. Nika isn't the most cooperative person."

"What have you been able to find out from Amanda Greer?" I asked Zachary.

"Nothing. She's gone. No one can find her. We've gotten a warrant and searched her house—not a soul there. I think it's safe to assume she's in Thailand and we may never see her again."

"I don't think so. Nika and Vega both told me Amanda never leaves the house."

"Maybe they're lying."

"I think Nika spends most of her life lying. But why would Vega lie? Actually, do you know if your team found a panic room at the Greers' house? When I met Vega, she said when threatened, Amanda would retreat into her panic room. I thought it was a metaphor when she said it. I mean, who has an actual panic room in their house?"

"I don't know, but I'd bet the Greers do. Let me get in touch with the officers who did the search and have them search again. We may need to get our hands on the blueprints to the house to find the room, which might take a little time."

"You could ask Vega. She'd know where to look."

"Good idea. I'll have them get in touch with her." While Zachary called his team, I went to put on my shoes. Coming in the bedroom door, I was faced with an enormous pink teddy bear. Oh dear! I really didn't want to explain the bear. I picked it up and turned to stuff it into my closet, but it was too late.

"Nice bear," Zachary said, smiling at me, his shoulder resting casually against the doorframe. "Where'd that come from?"

"I'm pretty sure you don't want to know." I tossed the stuffed atrocity on the bed. I'd have to figure out how to get rid of it some other time. I was certain Val would adore it.

Since I was far too wobbly to wear heels, I found my Mary Jane flats and slid them on. Zachary offered me his arm, and we headed out the door.

When we arrived at the Chanticleer Theater, he pulled up to the curb so I wouldn't have to walk too far. Like a true gentleman, Zachary came around the car to open the door for me and help me out. Yesler Square was crowded with people arriving and milling around outside the theater. It looked like there were going to be lots of people at the event, and that was a positive sign.

"Okay, you go in. I'll park and meet you inside. You're steady enough to make it on your own?" Zachary asked, helping me up the curb.

"I'm not made of glass, you know," I said. Even though I was feeling more fragile than usual, I could get used to all this extra attention.

Jaya was standing in the lobby, greeting people as they entered.

"Thanks very much for all your help on the gala. The entire HAT team is so happy with the work you and Tessa have done," Jaya said, beaming in her elegant burgundy dress. She was clearly happy the event, which had appeared on several occasions to be headed for disaster, was really happening.

"And thanks for talking with Mrs. Greer so we could keep our doors open for this event, and for *Hamlet* as well," Daniel said, looking dapper in his black suit and skinny emerald-colored tie.

"You're still going to open *Hamlet*?" I asked.

"As long as we can keep our lead actor out of jail," Daniel said, attempting a joke. "You can pick up your tickets at the box office."

I passed through the crowded lobby and made my way to the box office. I was astounded to find Vega helping customers at the service window.

"What are you doing here?" I asked.

"I thought maybe Daniel could use some help. After all, this auction was my dad's brainchild, so I thought someone from the family should be here. I knew I'd never get my mother to come, so here I am."

"I'm happy to see you," I said, smiling at Vega.

"Happy to be here. Here are your tickets," she said, handing them to me. "And good luck in the auction."

Zachary joined me in the lobby and we headed for our seats.

The place was packed, and I was hopeful that tonight we'd make a ton of money for the Homeless Advocacy Team. I found our seats in the front row—Tessa had made sure we had the best seats in the house. I was disappointed I wasn't backstage helping, but I knew that between Tessa, Val, and Uncle Freddie, the whole thing would run smoothly without me. Zachary settled into the seat next to me and draped his arm around me.

"Comfy?"

"Yep. Fingers crossed it all goes without a hitch."

"I got us a number for bidding." Zachary flashed a half-sheet of paper with the number 99 stamped on it.

"I hope I win something," I said, taking the paper from him.

With just seconds to go before the start of the event, Tessa's husband, Craig, slid into the seat next to me, their son Joey in tow. There was a still an open seat with a reserved sign on it on the other side of Zachary. The lights above us flashed, indicating everyone should take their seats. We spotted Bev coming down the center aisle. Zachary invited her to join us.

"Nice to see you, hon," Bev said, sitting down and reaching across Zachary to pat my knee.

I felt a tap on my shoulder and turned around to find Buff Brown sitting behind me next to Mr. Chu. I was glad to see both of them.

"Hi, Jax. Val told me about the auction. I thought I'd come and see if I could bid on something," Buff said. "Oh, and I donated a pet photography session to the auction. You saw the photos hanging on the walls in my office? They're all shots I took."

"I'm going to bid on that. I want some cat portraits," Mr. Chu said, clutching his bidding card. Buff could be busy for days taking photos if Mr. Chu won that auction item, given the large number of cats he kept.

"Oh, thank you for the little bronze chicken sculpture. Can you tell me more about it?" I asked Mr. Chu.

"It's an antique from Burma. You like it? It's just a decoration these days, but used to be for weighing opium."

"Wow. Thanks for telling me what it was, I had no idea." Given I'd been drugged with some sort of opioid earlier in the day, I wasn't too keen to learn that the sculpture had anything to do with the opium trade, but it was very thoughtful of him to bring me a gift. "I've already found a place to display it on the windowsill in my studio."

The lights dimmed, and I turned back around. A spotlight burst on, illuminating a figure on the stage. It was Val's Uncle Freddie, in full rock n roll regalia: red leather pants and a shiny black shirt, tall platform boots, and equally tall rock star hair.

"Good evening, everyone," Freddie shouted into the mic. "I'm Freddie Roberts, and I'll be your host tonight. So if everyone is ready, let's get this party started!" There was a blast of rock music, and the first model entered the stage. Freddie let us know what she was wearing, and he sounded pretty good. Val must have written up some descriptions of the outfits for him.

"Next we have Ashley, who is looking stunning in a lavender silk gown with an antique faux-amber necklace, courtesy of Chu's Antiquities. The necklace will be available for purchase during the auction later this evening." We all applauded as Ashley glided across the stage and twirled at all the right moments.

"Now, here's Izzy. She's looking fantastic in this emerald green tunic with bright stripes and black jeans. Finishing off this outfit is a black pendant with green and yellow accents, made by our very own Jax O'Connell." Everyone in the audience clapped, and several people around me patted me on the shoulder. The outfit and the coordinating necklace looked lovely, I just hoped the necklace would sell for a high dollar amount during the auction, for both HAT's sake and mine.

"Let's give a big round of applause for Izzy!" Freddie shouted, as he continued to whip the audience into a frenzy of appreciation for the models. The crowd roared again as Izzy came to the front of the stage, did a very professional spin and then exited into the wings.

All the rest of the girls, their outfits, and jewelry were stunning. They all looked incredibly poised and professional as they took the stage, each girl modeling two outfits during the fashion show part of the event. Tessa and I had done it. We pulled off the fashion show. Now we just needed to make it through the auction.

Everyone who had been working backstage came out onto stage with their pedestals—the ones we had been dragging around the first day of rehearsals. I noticed Ashley had taken over my position of placing a pedestal downstage left.

After the pedestals were in place, the stage filled with fog and all the models came out to take one last walk and a bow. But something was wrong. The girls looked bewildered and were staring off into the wings, looking for—or at—someone. I was puzzled to see that Izzy was not onstage with the rest of the girls. The fog was getting thicker and thicker. And then it hit me.

This was not fog. It was smoke.

"Zachary, we've got to get out of here."

"Are you not feeling well? I knew this was too much for you."

"No. Not just me. All of us. The theater is on fire. I swear to you."

"Jax, it's just fog."

"Smell it. Just stop and smell it," I said.

Zachary paused and took a deep breath. "I think you're right. Now, we can't cause a panic, you're not supposed to yell fire in a crowded theater," Zachary said, looking around for exit options.

Several people stood up in seats behind us, and there was a buzz of conversation through the crowd, as the audience sensed something was wrong.

"I just need to get to Tessa. She can stop the show," I said, rising from my seat and side stepping to the aisle.

Zachary told Bev to start an orderly evacuation. I told Craig the same thing.

"I'll call this into the fire department, then I'm headed for the fire alarm," Zachary said as he pulled out his phone and headed toward the lobby.

I went up the side steps and into the wings. The backstage was filling with smoke. I found Tessa. She'd just pulled the plug on the smoke machine and had figured out the smoke was coming from somewhere else.

"We've got to get everyone out of here. I think we've got the start of a fire somewhere," I said.

"I'll round up the girls and get them to the parking lot," Tessa said.

"Okay, and I'll make sure we get Val and Uncle Freddie. Anyone else we need to find back here?"

"No, but what about the audience?" she asked.

"We've got Craig and Bev in the audience to make sure everyone gets out safely. Zachary's calling the fire department. Be careful," I told her as she turned and headed off into the smoky darkness.

TWENTY-THREE

UNCLE FREDDIE tromped off the stage as the models exited on the other side with Tessa.

"What the hell is going on?" he asked me. "Can't we just turn off the damn smoke machine?"

"Tessa turned it off, but it looks like we've got something worse going on. I think we've got a fire in the building somewhere. We've got to evacuate. Can you go out and announce that everyone needs to get to an exit? We've got to get everyone out before the building bursts into flames, but we don't want anyone to panic and start a stampede."

Uncle Freddie strutted back out onto the stage.

"Weren't those young ladies fantastic? Another round of applause for our models. Now, we're having a little technical difficulty. Everyone, I'd like you to make your way out to Yesler Square through the lobby. I'm sure we'll be back in business again soon."

Just then the fire alarm sounded and the sprinklers started pouring down on our heads. The cat was out of the bag now, and a wave of panic rolled through the audience.

"Please, everyone," Freddie said, "just proceed calmly out of the building."

I found the lighting panel on the backstage wall and flipped all the switches. The backstage lights blinked on, as well as the lights in the audience.

Uncle Freddie found me backstage.

"Come on, we've got to get out of here," he said.

"Where's Val?" I asked.

"I don't know, she was with the girls on the other side of the stage," Freddie said. "I'm going to go see who is outside and make sure we know how many people you're looking for. We should have five girls, plus Tessa and Val, right?"

"Right." Val would be unhappy to hear she was not included as one of the girls. Having just turned forty, Val was no longer a girl, and I'd left that milestone in the dust several years ago.

I ran across the stage to search for anyone left behind. As I looked out into the audience, I was relieved to see the seating area was almost empty.

No one was in the dressing room. The door to the rehearsal space was open, so I headed for the stairs to search there. The smoke was thicker downstairs, and I wondered if this was where the fire had started. I clutched the handrail as I descended the staircase, feeling woozy as I went. I wasn't sure if that was leftover from the drugs I'd ingested or from the smoke I was inhaling. Stumbling into the rehearsal room, I found Val trying to coax Izzy out of the passage that led to the Underground.

"Come on, Izzy, we've got to get out of here!" Val shouted, reaching out to the girl.

"No, no, no," Izzy said, her hands covering her face. The alarm continued to blare. There were no sprinklers down here, so at least we were dry. "We can't leave without the guy I followed down here."

"What guy?"

"I dunno who it was but I was worried he might be coming down here to steal our stuff. My mom told us we could leave our regular clothes and backpacks in this room since there wasn't much space in the dressing room. But the guy I saw, he's not here."

Val grabbed one of Izzy's arms, and I grabbed the other and we pulled her through the door. Just then, I noticed someone moving in the darkness farther down the passageway.

"Val, you take Izzy to safety. I'll make my way out in a minute."

"No, Jax, you've got to come with us now," Val said, reaching out to me.

"I'll be fine. Now go!"

I turned and ran into the passageway, stumbling past the props and discarded set pieces. Up ahead I saw a figure frantically trying to ignite the box labeled *Pyro* with a book of matches. I recognized the costume—a hooded figure with a Venetian mask. I rushed toward the person, though I wasn't sure what I'd do once I reached him—or her. Throwing the matches on the ground, the culprit made a break for it, crashing onwards through the tunnel. I followed, but couldn't keep up the pace. I made it to the fork in the alleyway, where I'd been snooping just the other night. Which way had the person gone? Up into the box office, or beyond to who knows where?

I headed the only way I knew would take me out to the safety of the lobby. There was no way I wanted to get trapped in the other passage, since I didn't know whether it was a dead end or not. If I was lucky, whoever was down here with me was headed for the box office as well. Perhaps I'd find him there and Zachary could apprehend him. I huffed up the stairs and heaved open the door into the box office. It was empty. And wet. The sprinklers had stopped, but an alarm still wailed through the building. I let myself out into the lobby and burst out the front door breathing deep lungfuls of the crisp night air. I buckled over to catch my breath.

The fire trucks arrived and several firefighters jogged past me into the theater. I wanted to find Zachary and make sure everyone was safe. I walked slowly through the crowd of people gathered in the square. Just over a hundred people, all slightly damp and smelling faintly of smoke were standing in Yesler Square frightened and confused—but safe.

I had started the night out on the wimpy end of the spectrum—I'd never spent much time on the strong end—and was now exhausted. I found Zachary standing on a bench surveying the scene. He hopped down when he caught sight of me, took me in his arms, and held me tight.

"Thank goodness you're okay," he said. "You are okay, aren't you?" He released me, and wiped a little smudge of soot from my cheek.

"I'm fine, but you need to know—I saw a guy in the Underground—"

A firefighter interrupted me and pulled Zachary away to consult on the situation. When Zachary returned, he told me the fire had been extinguished but that there was still lingering smoke, and the floors and seats were soaked with water from the sprinklers. There was no way we were getting back into the theater. We hadn't even gotten to the most important part of the event, when we raised money for HAT during the auction. There was nothing left we could do. We had overcome so many obstacles, but we simply couldn't recover from this. All I wanted to do now was go home and crawl into bed.

Uncle Freddie found me in the crowd.

"So, what do you want to do?" he asked.

"Give up," I said. "I want to give up." I plopped myself onto a nearby bench, and put my head in my hands.

"We can't do that. We've got money to raise. Now, I think if we can gather everyone around over at the bandstand, I'll get up there and we'll keep going. What do you say?" Uncle Freddie wasn't going to give up.

"But some of our auction items are still inside. They're probably ruined by the smoke and water," I said.

"We're going to improvise," Freddie said, strutting off to find his helpers for the auction.

Moments later Uncle Freddie jumped on the bandstand stage to start the auction as if nothing had happened. He was a professional, through and through. Some of the volunteers, with the consent of the firefighters, rolled out a spotlight from the theater to give some much-needed light to Freddie on his makeshift stage.

"And now, as many of you know, we had a chandelier that we were going to auction off tonight," Freddie said. "Although the chandelier was destroyed in a tragic accident, the police have given us permission to auction what remains. For a good cause, of course." Just then, two uniformed officers appeared out of nowhere with two storage tubs full of glass pieces. I looked at Zachary, my mouth agape. "You said I couldn't have them."

"Well, you couldn't have them then, but we've got everything we need from them, so I pulled a few strings so we could release them."

"Wow. Thanks for doing that. I hope I win those bins of glass!" I really wanted them. Unfortunately, so did Tessa.

"Opening bid is $200," Uncle Freddie shouted.

Tessa raised her bidding card.

"We have a bid of $200 from bidder number 47."

She and I got into a ridiculous bidding war, with neither of us backing down. On and on we went, each of us upping the bid of the other. Finally, I stopped the madness.

"Tessa, please, let's stop. I'll split it with you, okay?"

Tessa nodded in agreement. I jumped up from the bench, waving my bidding card for what I hoped would be the last time.

"Going once, twice, sold! Sold to bidder number 66," Uncle Freddie shouted.

I realized my number was upside down.

"No, sorry! That's bidder number 99. My card was upside down," I shouted, flipping my card right side up.

"Sold to number 99, then," Uncle Freddie corrected as a volunteer approached me to get my contact and payment details.

"Whew!" I had won. I had grand plans for those bits and pieces. I planned to make a mosaic from some of the smaller pieces, and I hoped Tessa would want some of the larger pieces for a light fixture of her own, if we could put enough parts back together.

Uncle Freddie did an amazing job auctioning off all sorts of things that had been donated, including all the necklaces—five of which the models were wearing when they were evacuated. Uncle Freddie had even thrown in one of his old guitars, which fetched a hefty sum.

Buff bought a gift basket full of hair care products Val had donated as a last minute item. Given he didn't have a hair on his head, I wondered if those products would end up being used to shampoo dogs who might be under his care, or simply given to his receptionist, since he had no use for them. Mr. Chu was very pleased with himself, having been triumphant in the bidding war against Val for the pet photo shoot. Having lost the photo shoot, Val bid on and won the Thai silver necklace that had been donated by Amanda Greer.

By the end of the evening, we'd made a tidy sum for the Homeless Advocacy Team. It was a job well done, although we might have succeeded in making more had the chandelier been intact. Jaya from HAT was thrilled with the money we raised, and all the models, including Tessa's daughters, seemed happy to have participated in running a successful event.

I realized in all the commotion I still hadn't told Zachary about the man I'd seen in the Underground.

"I need to sit down for a bit," I told Zachary. I pointed to a bench at the end of the square, near the boutique where I'd bought my dress, away from the crowd so we could have some peace and quiet.

As we sat down, I glanced at the front windows of Cassie's shop. I saw the strangest thing. Daniel was inside the store, trying to break out through the newly-installed security gates. And he wasn't having much luck. I was sure he must have been who I'd seen in the Underground.

"See that man in the shop?" I asked Zachary pointing at the Styles by Cassie storefront.

"Yes."

"I think that's who started the fire. I chased him through the Underground, but lost sight of him. I came up through the box office, but the other passageway must lead to Cassie's boutique."

"How do you know so much about the tunnels under the theater?"

"I'm pretty sure you don't want to know."

"I'm pretty sure you're right," Zachary replied.

"I also think he might be the person who broke into my house the other night."

"Why do you think so?" he asked, his eyes focused on the frantic man, who looked like a caged animal as he paced back and forth behind the windows, trying to find a way out.

"Because the person I saw in the Underground was wearing the same thing as the burglar—a black hooded sweatshirt and a Venetian mask."

Zachary trotted off to talk with the firemen, who were wrapping things up in the theater lobby now that the fire had been extinguished. He took a small crew of firemen to Cassie's shop, where they used their gear to unlock the security gates and rescue Daniel.

He was acting much as he had when we first met him—like a complete and utter wreck. As I watched him, I was certain it was exactly that—an act. I was sure we'd find a hoodie and a mask somewhere in the Underground that belonged to him, as well as a matchbook with his DNA on it.

Getting up from the bench, I approached the group and pulled Zachary aside.

"You know how Austin scratched the letters MO on the stage before he died?" I asked. "We thought that meant it was Monika or Cassie Morton. But it wasn't MO. It was OW—Austin was trying to write Owens—Daniel Owens."

"How did you come to that conclusion?" Zachary asked.

"It was the auction bidding cards. You know how you said you got number 99? When I won the pieces of the Vega chandelier, Uncle Freddie thought I had number 66, and I had to correct him. It's all about perspective. We were reading Austin's message upside down."

"Interesting theory," Zachary said.

"To prove my theory you can check for any scratches on his Daniel's head. In case I'm very much mistaken, he's the burglar I interrupted in my house the other night who was ambushed by a kitten," I said.

"Gumdrop?" Zachary gave me a puzzled look. I had forgotten to tell him about the kitten.

"No, a tiny orange kitten that's been lurking around my back patio recently."

Zachary instructed one of the nearby police officers to arrest Daniel Owens.

"Why? What did I do?" Daniel howled as the officer cuffed him.

"Let's start with arson. From there, perhaps we'll consider you a suspect in the murder of Austin Greer," Zachary said as the officers hauled Daniel away.

"I want a lawyer. I'm not saying another thing until I see my lawyer," Daniel whimpered as the police escorted him to their squad car.

TWENTY-FOUR

AS WE SAT IN HIS CAR, Zachary leaned over and whispered in my ear.

"You're very brave," he said, kissing me gently on the lips.

"So are you," I replied, returning a kiss to him.

"I was going to give you this earlier, but I didn't have the chance," Zachary said, handing me a tiny box. Most women would have assumed it was a ring, but I knew better. He'd never propose to me while parked at Yesler Square.

"Should I open it?"

"Not now. But I hope you'll wear it."

Zachary drove me home and parked his car in front of my house. He walked me to the front door and kissed me goodnight. I yawned. I didn't mean to, but it happened.

"Do you want to—" I interrupted myself with another yawn. "I'm so sorry, I didn't mean—"

"You're tired. I think you're still recovering from whatever those drugs were that you ingested. With all the excitement of the evening, I think it's time for you to get some sleep. And while I'm tempted to come in and help you into bed, I think I'd be tempted to stay." He kissed me gently on the lips, holding me in an embrace longer than he ever had.

I yawned again. I couldn't deny it—I was exhausted.

"Get some sleep, and I'll talk with you tomorrow," he said, as he headed down my front steps, turning back and smiling as he went. I waved goodbye to him and shut the door. I ambled toward my bedroom, thinking about Zachary. A feeling of warmth flooded over me. Zachary was a terrific guy, even though he had a hard time expressing himself at times. My reverie was interrupted by the sound of Gummie meowing frantically. The sound was coming from my studio.

"What's up?" I asked my cat, entering the studio. I found him on my workbench, pacing back and forth in front the window, much as I'd seen Daniel do a little while ago.

"Yello, yellooooo, yeLLOOO," Gumdrop said.

I pulled back the blinds and looked out the window. Sitting on the window ledge outside was the orange kitten who had scared off the burglar the other night.

"Yello?" Gummie repeated.

"Is this little kitty bothering you, Gummie? Is this why you've been so out of sorts?" The window was open a crack. There was a screen in place, so Gummie couldn't have escaped through the opening.

What I wasn't sure about was how Gummie felt about the kitten. Was he trying to tell me something? Either good or bad? Concerned the kitten was out at night, and wasn't safe, I wanted to try to get her into the house. I was worried I might spook her if I opened the door. I went to the kitchen and put a few spoons of tuna into a bowl. I brought it back and put it on the workbench. The kitten eagerly sniffed at the screen. Gently and slowly, I opened the window a little further, exposing more of the screen. All the while, Gumdrop paced back and forth, meowing.

I found a razor blade on my worktable and cut open the screen, creating an opening for the kitten, who, motivated by the smell of the tuna, scampered in through the hole. While the kitten chowed down on the tuna, I slid the window shut. Gumdrop, who was usually not very nice to anyone who he saw as an invader—such as potential boyfriends and basset hounds—seemed smitten with the little orange cat. He walked back and forth next to the kitten, meowing in his distinctive way.

"Yello, yello, yellooooo."

"This little kitten isn't yellow, Gummie," I said, picking up the kitten who had finished eating and whose belly was now swollen to about the size and tautness of a tennis ball. "She's orange, or more like ginger. That's what I'll call her—Ginger—at least until we find her owner."

I understood now why Gummie had been sick. The kitten sneezed. As I looked into Ginger's eyes, I saw the same discharge I'd seen in Gumdrop's. She must've infected him by passing her germs through the window screen.

"I need to take you to see Dr. Brown," I said to the kitten. I'd heard Buff's motorcycle pull up out front a few minutes earlier, so I was pretty sure Buff was next door with Val. I hoped I wouldn't be interrupting anything. Gumdrop was at my heels, following me to the door as I carried the kitten through the house.

"Sorry, Gummie, you don't get to come with us," I said, opening my front door.

I knocked on Val's door. When she answered, her hair was a little messy and her lipstick smudged.

"Maybe I should come back later," I said, backing away from the door and ready to bolt back inside my house with Ginger.

"Oh, no, it's okay. We're, um, not doing anything that can't be interrupted."

I didn't want to know. Okay, I did want to know. I peered over Val's shoulder. Buff was playing tug-o-war with Stanley on the carpet.

"Stanley's getting acquainted with Buff," Val said, smoothing her hair down a little, though it bounced back up as soon as she removed her hand. "What have you got there?"

"This kitten's been hanging around my back door, and Gummie seems to adore her."

"Aw, she—or he—is adorable," Val said, tickling the kitten under the chin with her long, red nails. "Oh, but I think she might be sick. Look at the yucky stuff in her eyes."

Buff joined us at the door. He took the kitten from me, then he gave it a quick look under the tail.

"You can safely say 'she,'" he said. "Oh, and the poor baby has a cold. No wonder Gumdrop ended up with it. They've clearly been hanging out together."

"Yes, I think they've been talking through the window screen," I said.

Stanley, upset that Buff had given up the game with him, started bounding around the room. It was also possible that he smelled the kitten.

"I think he wants to see the kitten," Val said.

"Well, I think we'd best wait until she's well before for we introduce her to Stanley," Buff said.

"What should I do now?" I asked.

"We need to see if this kitten has an ID chip. Bring her round to the office tomorrow and I'll scan her. If there's no chip, then I think it's safe to say she's a stray. You could take her down to animal control, or hold on to her and put up some signs and post on Craigslist if you want to find her a home."

"And if I want to keep her?"

"If you try to find the owner, and one doesn't show up, she's all yours. Then you'll need to bring her in for shots and she'll need to be spayed. The eye drops I gave you for Gumdrop—you can use them on her as well. Have you got a name for this little pipsqueak?"

"I'm thinking about calling her Ginger."

"She is a ginger color," Buff agreed.

As I got ready to head back to my side of the duplex, Val handed me a familiar box. It was the donation from Amanda Greer that Val had won in the auction.

"Do you think you could fix this necklace for me?"

"Sure, that's easy. What's wrong with it?"

"It's a little too long for me. Maybe you can make it a little shorter, and I wouldn't mind if you could make it a little more sparkly." Of course, she wanted more sparkle.

"Sure, Val, I'm happy to fix it."

With the box in one hand and a kitten in the other, I headed back to my side of the duplex. I didn't really need a kitten, but it seemed to me that Gumdrop did, and I was happy to oblige.

TWENTY-FIVE

ZACHARY CALLED the next day to check on me, but what I really wanted to know was what had happened with Daniel.

"We got a full confession. It took a while to get the truth out of him. He was a convincing actor, but then again, we have some excellent interrogators. Daniel knew about the drugs Nika was bringing into the country. She had confided in him about where the money was coming from that paid his salary. Austin had realized things were not as they seemed. He had threatened to take the whole thing to the police, but he didn't want his wife to end up in prison for drug trafficking, so he didn't do anything right away. Daniel knew if Austin went to the police that the theater would shut down."

"But with Austin dead, wasn't that likely as well?" I asked.

"Yes, I suppose so, but it was a risk he was willing to take. Especially since he had Nika on the inside, who was able to talk with Amanda Greer and could convince her to keep the theater open in Austin's memory. You see, Nika really had control of the whole thing."

"But who killed Austin? Was it Nika?"

"No, Daniel confessed. And I think he was rather impressed with himself about how he did it and proud of how well he pulled off the distressed theater employee act."

Ugh! I wanted to strangle that rat for fooling us. But, I assumed he'd be getting his just desserts in prison.

"So, how did he hit Austin with the chandelier—that must've been next to impossible to orchestrate."

"Daniel would wait every night in the technician's booth for Austin to place the ghost light in a particular spot on the stage. Daniel had marked the spot with a piece of glow-in-the-dark tape, so Austin could place it in exactly the right spot. On the night he murdered Austin, Daniel moved the tape so it was directly below the chandelier, then climbed into the lighting grid above the stage and waited for Austin to roll the ghost light into position. Then he released the cable and its safety chain."

"Such a gruesome way to go."

"That's for sure. And he left that night through the Underground, coming out through Cassie's shop. That way, anyone who lingered in the parking lot after the rehearsal wouldn't see him leave. And he could be the first to arrive the following morning and discover the body."

"And that's what caught Daniel off guard—he didn't know Cassie had installed security gates that would make it impossible for him to make that escape again. But why would he want to burn down the theater? I don't get it," I said.

"He was spooked when the Greers' daughter, Vivian, or Vega as she's known these days, showed up the night of the auction. She knew her way around the theater, and Daniel was certain she'd find his records, which he'd stored in a box marked *Pyro* in their lower level storage area," Zachary said.

"Dammit! I saw the box labeled *Pyro*, and even saw him try to light it on fire. I thought it had fireworks inside—I would never have thought to look inside."

"Apparently Daniel was trying to destroy the records before Vega found them. He was certain that if Vega understood what he and Nika had been doing with the drug smuggling, she'd go to the police."

"So, did he confess to breaking into my house?" I asked.

"He did. But ultimately, since nothing went missing, and there are so many other crimes committed, that's the least of Daniel's worries."

"How did he even know where I lived?"

"Nika had your address. It's on your business card. You might want to think about getting a P.O. box so random people aren't showing up at your door in the future," he said.

"So it was Nika and Daniel working together?"

"Daniel has pretty much thrown Nika under the bus, saying it was all her idea to kill Austin Greer. She was the one smuggling the drugs. Daniel was simply the one funneling the money into the theater, and of course, is responsible for Mr. Greer's death, though he says he was just following her orders."

"I don't think Daniel is as innocent as he's pretending to be."

"Me neither, but it will come out in court, someday," Zachary said.

"Did you find Amanda Greer?" I asked.

"We did. She was in her panic room, like you thought she might be. So, kudos to you, Jax."

"And did you find the drugs in the panic room too?"

"No. We didn't find a thing."

•   •   •

I got a call from Bev Marley the Monday after the auction.

"I want to thank you for helping me with my investigation," she said.

"I don't think I helped that much, but, you're welcome," I said.

"We've still got some work to do to obtain their financial data, but it looks like there's a long history of the Greers buying expensive items and then turning around and donating them to nonprofits. Then they'd take massive write-offs on their business and personal taxes. That's not what I expected to find—it's not money laundering per se, but tax fraud is still a crime."

"But what about the drugs? Did you find them?"

"Sorry, Jax, we searched the house and the warehouse and found nothing."

"Look, I know what Nika said. She and Amanda were bringing heroin in from Thailand."

"We didn't get a confession from Amanda. She seemed like she came clean on everything and didn't know anything about drugs. Maybe Nika lied to you? Criminals do lie," Bev said.

"Can't you talk with Nika and get some answers? She got the drugs from somewhere because she'd been giving them to Austin, and she gave them to me, too."

"Nika's gotten herself some lawyers, and she's not saying much at this point. Well, hon, it's been nice working with you. You've been a real pro. Hope to see you around." Bev wished me well and hung up.

Back in my studio, I found the box with Val's new necklace in it. I pulled the piece from the box. It was beautiful. As I held it up, I realized it wasn't as I remembered it. This piece seemed lighter to me, and the beads didn't look quite like what I recalled were in the piece Amanda had given me. I'd only seen the necklace up close when I first received it and again when I put it on my worktable, so my memory of it could be wrong. I wondered if the strand could have somehow been swapped. It had been at my house since I'd gotten it from Amanda. While I was at the hospital it had been transported to the theater, and it could have been swapped out at any point before the auction started. If I were to guess, I'd say Daniel swapped the necklaces the night he broke into my house—assuming I wasn't simply forgetting what the necklace looked and felt like.

Ginger curled up in the necklace box—in the most inconvenient place. I had forgotten how silly a kitten could be. I placed her in a spot of sunshine on the other end of my workbench near Gumdrop. Instead of curling up next to Gummie, Ginger jumped on him. He opened a single eye and gave the kitten an impatient glare, then fell back asleep.

I spotted the gift Mr. Chu had given me sitting on the windowsill. I remembered that he told me it was an opium weight. The words *opium weight* reverberated in my head. Of course opium had a weight, as all substances do. Sitting next to the opium weight was the tiny whale carving I had found in my great-aunt's trunk. I recalled Buff's words, and my frequent advice to Val: You need to look on the inside to find what really matters.

I recalled Nika had been hesitant to give the necklace to me. I wondered if the difference in the weight of the necklace I had and the necklace Amanda had initially given was because the first one was full of opium. There was one way to find out.

I called Bev.

"Do you think we could get into Amanda Greer's warehouse? I think I know where to find the drugs," I said when she answered.

"Jax, we've had all sorts of professionals in there. We didn't find anything," Bev said.

"Can you just humor me?" I asked.

"Sure, hon. Meet you there in an hour."

As I got ready to go, I reached in my purse and found the tiny box Zachary had given me. I opened it and peeked inside. I wasn't sure why Zachary thought I needed it, but he told me to wear it, and I was happy to oblige. I had a little work to do before I left to see Bev.

•   •   •

Bev and I arrived at the Greers' house at the same time, and we headed to the back gate where the warehouse was located. She unlocked the gate, and soon we were inside the converted carriage house where Amanda stored her beads. Everything looked more or less as it had the last time I was there.

I headed straight to the small room where I had seen the necklaces with the large beads and where Amanda had pulled the necklace to give to me.

"See these? If I'm not very much mistaken, this is where we'll find the drugs." I picked up a strand of ten beads, each an inch and a half in diameter. They were heavy, as I'd expected.

I placed the strand on the floor and stepped hard on one of the beads, much like what Nika had done when she'd crushed the mic

Bev had given me. The bead popped in half, revealing a sticky white powder inside.

"That's the stuff," Bev said, with a smile. "Thanks for finding it. And now that you have, I want to say it's been nice knowing you, Jax." Bev pushed me roughly against the wall, knocking the wind out of me.

What the hell was going on?

"Do you have any idea what the street value of these drugs is?" Bev asked.

"Uh, no, but, it doesn't really matter, right? Because they're only going to be evidence in a case against Amanda Greer, Daniel, and Nika, right?"

"Oh, I don't think so. I think we're going to find the money I make selling this crap to one of my friends on the street is going to mean early retirement for me," Bev said.

"You won't get away with it. Not now that I know because—"

She pulled a gun from her purse, and placed the barrel under my chin.

"I'd be thinking otherwise if I were you, hon," Bev said with a sinister gleam in her eyes. "Now, I'm going to take the gun away, and you're going to listen to me real carefully."

"Okay," I squeaked.

"You're going to help me load all of these beads into my car, and then maybe you'll live. Or, maybe I'll have to kill you after I discover you here at the Greer household trying to steal some valuables."

"Or maybe, you can drop your weapon." Zachary stepped through the door with his gun drawn. "Bev, put the gun down. Now."

"Hey, my boy Zee," Bev said. "I discovered Jax trying to steal—"

"Sorry. It's not going to work. I heard the whole thing."

"Heard it? How?"

"Like my nice boutonnière? After my last one got crushed, Zachary supplied me with a new one. Of course, I had to decorate it up like the old one."

"Crap," Bev said, slowly setting her gun on the ground.

"Now kick it over to me," Zachary said. She did as she was told, grumbling as she did.

"We've been watching you for a while, Bev. So many of your cases were ending up without closure. I've been working with the state on an internal investigation. Looks like we were right about you."

"You know what it's like to have worked all your life doing something you don't care about only to realize you've not even made any decent money at it? It sucks, knowing I'm facing retirement and have little to show for it."

"I don't think you'll have to worry about retirement anymore," Zachary said. "Time to go." Zachary picked up the gun from the cement floor and guided Bev into the back seat of his black sedan.

"Nice work, Jax. Can you stick around until my backup team can get here and secure those beads with the drugs inside them?"

"Sure thing."

I wandered back into the carriage house to wait for the police to arrive. Walking between the rows of tables, I ran my hands over the strands of beads. They were beautiful. I wondered what would happen to them. I thought about Vega. Although she had severed ties with her parents, I supposed she would somehow be involved in her parents' estate at this point. I wasn't sure what would happen to Amanda. A lot would depend on whether she was truly uninvolved in the drug smuggling operation.

TWENTY-SIX

VEGA CALLED me a few days later to let me know she'd finished the glass light fixture she'd made me, and we set a time for her to come over. She arrived with a cardboard box, and I took her into my attic.

Vega looked around the new, improved attic. "Hey, your room turned out really nice. I think this light is going to work great in here," Vega said, pulling out the glass dome light. It was perfect. The mottled colors of purple, blue, and green glowed brilliantly even without being illuminated. "I think I'm going to have to make some more."

"Oh! It's gorgeous," I said, marveling at the colors. "Thank you."

"You want me to put it up for you?" Vega asked.

"No, that's okay. I've got a contractor coming over to finish up my attic renovation. He can install it. What do I owe you?"

"No charge. You did a lot to help figure out what had happened to my father. Think of this as a thank you," Vega said. She spotted the bin of broken glass that had once been her spectacular chandelier.

"Ah, hell. I know what that is," Vega said.

"Yeah, it's the remains of your chandelier."

"What are you going to do with all these pieces?" She asked, picking up a shard to examine it.

"I haven't quite figured that out yet, but I was thinking about making a mosaic backsplash in my kitchen, if that's okay with you. This was your work, before it got destroyed. I wouldn't want to do anything with it you didn't approve of."

"I hope something beautiful comes from all those bits and pieces. Let me know when you've finished your project. I'd love to see it. I think it'll be a little like my life—you know, it's been broken to pieces, but I'm hoping to reassemble it into something beautiful and unexpected."

"I hope so, too. Can you tell me what happened?" I asked. "I feel like I'm still missing some pieces."

"Look, I'm not entirely sure. No one is talking to me, other than my mother. It seems she was pretty clueless about what was going on. She and I had a long, tearful reunion. I'm sure it's just the first of many conversations we need to have. And we need each other for support, especially now that my father is gone."

I was glad to hear Vega had reconciled with her mother and I hoped that together they would be able to put their lives back together.

"Nika was bringing the drugs into the country in the larger finished necklaces, right?"

"Yes, and she only gave my mother the clean beads to work with," Vega said.

"So, you mother is innocent?"

"Looks like it. She's going to have to figure out if she can make ends meet by selling her beads and her jewelry. My mother has promised to get some treatment for her agoraphobia. She's got some tax trouble, but we're working on figuring that out. I think we'll be able to find a way for her to stay afloat. We may not have to sell the Chanticleer Theater, but we're thinking about converting it into low-income housing. There's some water and smoke damage, so it's time to renovate, and we might as well do it right."

"I'm sure the Homeless Advocacy Team would be excited about that," I said, taking a seat on the top step of the attic stairs. Vega joined me.

"I agree. It's better than any donation we can give them."

"Do you know what happened to the drugs once Nika got them?"

"Looks like she sold them and then deposited the money into my parents' account, telling my mother how successful she'd been at selling the beads to her avid buyers. My mother didn't question it. She was just happy her bead importing business was doing so well. Daniel Owens took the donations from my dad when the theater was having cash flow problems. Dad spent it on all sorts of things—like buying that chandelier and then donating it. He wasn't evil, just clueless. Nika was really the evil one in all of this. She'd done so much to manipulate my mother. In my mind, she's the one who was the culprit. And you brought her down—so, thank you."

TWENTY-SEVEN

THE NEXT DAY Rudy was scheduled to come over to wrap up the attic renovation. There was a knock at the door, and I was surprised to discover Ryan standing in front of me with tickets in one hand.

"Ryan! What are you doing here?" I asked.

"I wanted to invite you and Zachary to the opening night of *Hamlet*," he said, passing me the tickets.

"*Hamlet*? I thought it was canceled. Isn't the Chanticleer Theater closed due to smoke and water damage?"

"It is. We decided to do what you did with the auction and move the show out to the bandstand in Yesler Square. The cast and crew salvaged what we could of the set and the costumes. Our first show is tomorrow evening. I'm hoping you'll come."

"Oh, sure, Ryan, I wouldn't miss it for the world. Maybe I can bring Val and her new boyfriend, too," I said as I realized he'd given me four tickets.

"Great. Well, I hope to see you tomorrow. Oh, and bring your own chair since the square doesn't have any seating." Ryan sauntered off, as sexy as ever. But, he was not tempting to me in the least. I loved Zachary. And that was a surprising feeling to have, and one I'd not expected to ever feel again after breaking up with Jerry while I was still in Miami. I hadn't told Zachary how I felt yet, but I knew I needed to. And I hoped he felt the same way.

I busied myself in the studio, thinking about Zachary and all that had happened. I was looking forward to getting back into my routine of making and selling handmade glass beads, now that the gala and its chaos was finally over. Rudy arrived as I was packing up the beads I'd made him.

"So, what do you think of the finished room?" he asked, as we admired the newly renovated attic.

"It's perfect. Thanks so much for working on it. You and Dylan did a superb job," I said, handing him a pouch full of tiny alien and spaceship beads, part of his payment for remodeling my attic.

"Hey, thanks. You know, Dylan's going to work out really well for me. I may have to steal him from Tessa."

"Don't you dare. She'll never forgive me."

Rudy laughed his deep rumble of a laugh, as he gathered his tools together to take down to his truck.

"Oh, hey, I found this when I was working on your floor. It was wedged under one of the loose floorboards I had to remove." Rudy handed me a slender cedar box. "Sorry, I forgot all about it, what with you ending up in the hospital, the auction, and the fire at the theater—too many things going on."

I took the box. It had a small keyhole on its front side, and I had a feeling I had the key for it nestled inside an ivory carving of a whale. I couldn't wait for Rudy to leave so I could open the box. He grabbed the last of his tools and headed out the door.

"Thanks for everything," I said, closing the door behind him. I dashed to the windowsill and grabbed the tiny whale carving. Joined by Gumdrop and Ginger, I headed up the attic stairs. My new attic, which had revealed these treasures in the first place, was the right place to open the box. I sat down on the floor, and I laid the box in front of me. I pulled the tail from the small sculpture, and the key dropped from its hiding place into my hand. Slowly, I pressed the key into the lock, and the box popped open.

I carefully pulled a yellowed paper from the box and unfolded it on the floor next to me. It was a deed for a property near Port Angeles, Washington.

I'd never heard my great-aunt talk about any property other than this one. Did she own land on the Olympic Peninsula at the time of her death? If so, did that mean it was mine? And why would she have kept it a secret? I didn't have any answers, but I was certain I would find them, along with other treasures along the way.

Gumdrop crawled into my lap, with Ginger wedging herself in, too. In my glorious new room, these two cats, my friends, and my family were my most valuable treasures of all. I didn't need to hunt any further, at least not today.

ACKNOWLEDGMENTS AND NOTES FROM THE AUTHOR

This book is dedicated to my brilliant and beautiful daughter Kiera. She and I spent most of our spare time at a local community theater while she was in her teens. Some of the inspiration for this story comes from my work at the theater, though I can assure you no one died from a chandelier crashing down upon them during my tenure.

Perhaps you have wondered how I came up with the name Gumdrop for Jax's cat. One of Kiera's many nicknames is Gumdrop. Yes, I named a fictional cat after my daughter, though their personalities are quite different. Gumdrop was inspired by my beloved Willow Cat as well as a fluffy-footed gray chicken we once had.

I'd like to give a round of applause to all the early readers of this book. I couldn't have done it without their insightful feedback when I needed it most.

My talented editor, Ellen Margulies, deserves a standing ovation for her attention to detail, her humor, and her ability to push me toward the best story I can write.

And last, but certainly not least, a humongous thank-you to my husband, Jeff, for his unwavering faith in me, as well as the chocolate chip cookies he bakes during times of stress.

ABOUT THE AUTHOR

Janice Peacock decided to write her first mystery novel after working in a glass studio full of colorful artists who didn't always get along. They reminded her of the quirky and often humorous characters in the murder mystery books she loves to read. Inspired by that experience, she combined her two passions and wrote *High Strung*, the first book in the Glass Bead Mystery Series featuring glass beadmaker Jax O'Connell.

When Janice isn't writing about glass artists-turned-amateur-detectives, she creates glass beads using a torch, designs one-of-a-kind jewelry, and makes sculptures using hot glass. Her work has been exhibited internationally and is in the permanent collections of the Corning Museum of Glass, the Glass Museum of Tacoma, WA, and in private collections worldwide.

Janice lives in the San Francisco Bay Area with her husband, two cats, and an undisclosed number chickens. She has a studio full of beads...lots and lots of beads.

CONNECT WITH JANICE PEACOCK

www.JanicePeacock.com
jp@janicepeacock.com
www.blog.janicepeacock.com

Sign up for Janice's newsletter:
www.tinyurl.com/janpeacnewsletter

www.facebook.com/janpeac
Twitter, Instagram: @JanPeac
www.pinterest.com/janpeac
www.JanicePeacockGlass.com

Did you enjoy this book?
Please write a review on the website where you purchased it.

MORE BOOKS IN THE GLASS BEAD MYSTERY SERIES

HIGH STRUNG
GLASS BEAD MYSTERY SERIES
BOOK ONE

After inheriting a house in Seattle, Jax O'Connell is living the life of her dreams as a glass beadmaker and jewelry designer. When she gets an offer to display her work during a bead shop's opening festivities, it's an opportunity Jax can't resist—even though the store's owner is the surliest person Jax has ever met.

The weekend's events become a tangled mess when a young beadmaker is found dead nearby and several oddball bead enthusiasts are suspects. Jax must string together the clues to clear her friend Tessa's name—and do it before the killer strikes again.

Also available in audio book and ebook formats.

A BEAD IN THE HAND
GLASS BEAD MYSTERY SERIES
BOOK TWO

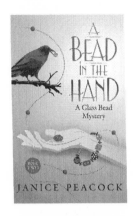

A bead bazaar turns bizarre when jewelry designer and glass beadmaker Jax O'Connell discovers a dead body beneath her sales table. Suspected of murder, Jax and her friend Tessa scramble to find the killer among the fanatic shoppers and eccentric vendors. They have their hands full dealing with a scumbag show promoter, hipsters in love, and a security guard who wants to do more than protect Jax from harm. Adding to the chaos, Jax's quirky neighbor Val arrives unexpectedly with trouble in tow. Can Jax untangle the clues before she's arrested for murder?

Also available in audio book and ebook formats.

OFF THE BEADIN' PATH
GLASS BEAD MYSTERY SERIES
BOOK THREE

Glass beadmaker Jax O'Connell and her friend Tessa have no idea what challenges await them when they take a glassblowing class with Marco De Luca, a famous Italian glass artist—and infamous lothario.

After the first night of class, Tessa sees a body through the rain-streaked window of the studio. The next morning there's no sign of Marco, and one of the studio owners is also missing. The local sheriff isn't taking the disappearances seriously, but Tessa knows what she saw. To complicate matters, Officer Shaw and Detective Grant are both vying for Jax's attention as she tracks down clues in a small town that's been keeping more than one secret.

Jax and Tessa must face their fears to find the body and uncover the killer before another life is shattered.

Also available in audio book and ebook formats.

BE STILL MY BEADING HEART
A GLASS BEAD MINI-MYSTERY

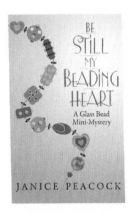

It's Valentine's Day and Jax O'Connell's red VW bug is missing. Did she forget where she parked the Ladybug as she rushed to deliver her handmade glass beads, or has the beloved car been stolen? Searching the streets of Seattle, Jax and her best friend, Tessa, face some unsavory characters. Jax regrets not having a date on the most romantic day of the year after spotting Ryan, Seattle's newest--and hottest--cop and running into Zachary, the stern yet sexy detective. She must take matters into her own hands to find the Ladybug and salvage her love life, and do it before the day is over. SPECIAL BONUS MATERIAL: Included with this short story are sample chapters from High Strung, Book 1 in the Glass Bead Mystery Series.

Find retailers for the Glass Bead Mystery Series at
www.janicepeacock.com/books.html

Made in the USA
Middletown, DE
23 March 2019